AUTOPOF

also by Edouard Levé in English translation

Suicide

AUTOPORTRAIT
Edouard Levé

translated by Lorin Stein

DALKEY ARCHIVE PRESS
CHAMPAIGN | DUBLIN | LONDON

Originally published in French as *Autoportrait* by P.O.L éditeur, 2005
Copyright © 2005 by P.O.L éditeur
Translation copyright © 2012 by Lorin Stein
First edition, 2012
All rights reserved

Library of Congress Cataloging-in-Publication Data

Levé, Édouard.
  [Autoportrait. English]
  Autoportrait / Edouard Leve ; translated by Lorin Stein. -- 1st ed.
     p. cm.
  "Originally published in French as Autoportrait by P.O.L. editeur, 2005."
  ISBN 978-1-56478-707-1 (pbk. : alk. paper)
  I. Stein, Lorin. II. Title.
  PQ2712.E87Z4613 2012
  843'.92--dc23

                              2011041213

Partially funded by a grant from the Illinois Arts Council, a state agency, and by the
University of Illinois at Urbana-Champaign

Cet ouvrage publié dans le cadre du programme d'aide à la publication bénéficie du
soutien du Ministère des Affaires Etrangères et du Service Culturel de l'Ambassade de
France représenté aux Etats-Unis

Cet ouvrage a bénéficié du soutien des Programmes d'aide á la publication de
Culturesfrance/Ministère français des affaires étrangères et européennes

This work received support from the French Ministry of Foreign Affairs and the Cultural
Services of the French Embassy in the United States through their publishing assistance
program

This work, published as part of a program of aid for publication, received support from
CulturesFrance and the French Ministry of Foreign Affairs

www.dalkeyarchive.com

Cover: design and composition by Danielle Dutton, illustration by Edouard Levé
Printed on permanent/durable acid-free paper and bound in the United States of America

When I was young, I thought *Life A User's Manual* would teach me how to live and *Suicide A User's Manual* how to die. I have spent three years and three months abroad. I prefer to look to my left. I have a friend who gets off on betrayal. The end of a trip leaves me with a sad aftertaste, the same as the end of a novel. I forget things I don't like. I may have spoken, without knowing it, to someone who killed someone. I look down dead-end streets. I am not afraid of what comes at the end of life. I don't really listen to what people are saying. I am surprised when someone gives me a nickname and we hardly know each other. I am slow to notice when someone mistreats me, it's always so surprising: evil is somehow unreal. I archive. I spoke to Salvador Dalí when I was two. Competition does not drive me. To describe my life precisely would take longer than to live it. I wonder if I will turn reactionary with age. When I sit with bare legs on vinyl, my skin doesn't slide, it squeaks. I have cheated on two women, I told them, one didn't care, one did. I joke about death. I do not love myself. I do not hate myself. I do not forget to forget. I do not believe in the existence of Satan. My rap sheet is clean. I wish a season lasted a week. I would rather be bored alone than with someone else. I wander empty places and eat in deserted restaurants. When it comes to food, I prefer the savory to the sweet, the raw to the cooked, the hard to the soft, the cold to the hot, the aromatic to the odorless. I cannot sit still and write unless there is food in the refrigerator. I can easily go without drinking or smoking. In a foreign country, I hesitate to laugh when my interlocutor burps while we are talking. I notice gray hair on people too young to have it. It's better for me not to read medical textbooks, especially passages describing the symptoms of some illness: no sooner do I find out one exists than I detect it in myself. War seems so unreal to me I have trouble believing my father was in one. I have seen a man who expressed one thing with the left side of his face and something else with the right. I am not sure I love New

York. I do not say "A is better than B" but "I prefer A to B."
I never stop comparing. When I am coming back from a
trip, the best part isn't going through the airport or getting home, but the taxi ride in between: you're still traveling, but not really. I sing badly, so I don't sing. Because I
am funny people think I'm happy. I want never to find an
ear in a meadow. I am no fonder of words than of a hammer or a vise. I do not know the green boys. In the store
windows of English-speaking countries, I read the word
sale (dirty) in French. I cannot sleep beside someone who
moves around, snores, breathes heavily, or steals the covers. I can sleep with my arms around someone who
doesn't move. I had an idea for a Dream Museum. I have
a tendency, because it's easier, to call people "friends" who
aren't, I can't think of another word for people whom I
know and like but with whom I have no special connection. On the train, facing backward, I don't see things
coming, only going. I am not saving for my retirement. I
consider the best part of the sock to be the hole. I do not
keep track of how much money is in my bank account.
My bank account is rarely in the red. *Shoah*, *Numéro zéro*,
Mobutu King of Zaïre, *E.R.*, *Titicut Follies*, and *La Conquete
de Clichy* have affected me more than the best works of

fiction. The ready-made films of Jean-Marc Chapoulie have made me laugh harder than the best comedies. I have attempted suicide once, I've been tempted four times to attempt it. The distant sound of a lawn mower in summer brings back happy childhood memories. I am bad at throwing. There was a compulsive collector in my family, at her death they found a shoebox labeled in painstaking calligraphy: "Little bits of string that have no use." I do not believe the wisdom of the sages will be lost. I once tried to make a book-museum of vernacular writing, it reproduced handwritten messages from unknown people, classed by type: flyers about lost animals, justifications left on windshields for parking cops so as to avoid putting money in the meter, desperate appeals for witnesses, announcements of a change in management, office messages, home messages, messages to oneself. I have thought, listening to an old man tell me his life story, "This man is a museum of himself." I have thought, listening to the son of an American black radical talk, "This man is a ready-made." I have thought, seeing a man who had wasted away, "This man is a ghost of himself." My parents went to the movies every Friday night until they got a TV. I like the straightforward sound of a paper bag but not of a plastic bag, which fidgets. I have heard but never seen fruit fall from the branch. Proper names fascinate me because I don't know what they mean. I have a friend who, when he has people over for dinner, never sets out serving dishes but arranges the food on plates like a restaurant, so there's no way to have seconds. I have lived for several years without insurance. I sometimes feel uneasier around a nice person than a mean one. My worst memories of traveling are funnier in the telling than my good ones. It disconcerts me that a child should address me as "monsieur." A swingers' club was the first place I ever saw people make love in front of me. I have not masturbated in front of a woman. I masturbate less to pictures than to memories. I have never regretted saying what I really thought. Love stories bore me. I never tell my own. I don't talk much about women I go out with, but I like hearing my friends talk about the women they go out with. A woman came to meet me in a distant country after a month and a half apart, I hadn't missed her, within seconds I realized I didn't love her anymore. In India, I traveled in a train compartment with a Swiss man whom I didn't know, we were crossing the plains of Kerala, I told him more about myself in several hours than I had told my best friends in several years, I knew I would never see him again, he was an ear without repercussions. I have sometimes been suspicious. Looking at old photos leads me to believe that the body evolves. I reproach others for what they reproach in me. I am not stingy, I admire money well spent. I like certain uniforms not as symbols, but for their functional sobriety. I will sometimes announce good news, concerning myself, to someone I like and be shocked to realize that he's jealous. I would not like to have famous parents. I am not handsome. I am not ugly. From certain angles, tanned and wearing a black shirt, I can find myself handsome. I find myself ugly more often than handsome. The times I find myself handsome are not the times I'd like to be. I find myself uglier in profile than straight on. I like my eyes, my hands, my forehead, my ass, my arms, my skin, I do not like my thighs, my elbows, my chin, my ears, the curve at the back of my neck, my nostrils from below, I have no opinion about my dick. My face is asymmetrical. The left side of my face looks nothing like the right. I like my voice after a night out or when I have a cold. I don't need anything. I am not looking to seduce a wearer of Birkenstocks. I do not like the big toe. I wish I had no nails. I wish I had no beard to shave. I have no interest in awards, I have no respect for distinctions, I don't care what I'm paid. I am drawn to strange people. I feel sympathy for the unlucky. I do not like paternalism. I feel more at ease with the old than with the young. I can ask endless questions of people I think I will never see again. Some day I will wear black cowboy boots with a purple velvet suit. To me the smell of manure recalls a bygone era, whereas the smell of wet earth evokes no particular time. I can't remember the name of a person I've just met. I'm not ashamed of my family, but I do not invite them to my openings. I have often been in love. I love myself less than I have been loved. I am surprised when someone loves me. I do not consider myself handsome just because a woman thinks so. My intelligence is uneven. My amorous states resemble each other, and those of other people, more than my works resemble each other, or those of other people. I find something pleasant in the pain of a fading love. I have never had a shared bank account. A friend once remarked that I seem glad when guests show up at my house but also when they leave. I begin more than I finish. I show up at people's houses more easily than I leave. I do not know how to interrupt an interlocutor who bores me. I will gorge on an all-you-can-eat buffet to the point of nausea. I have good digestion. I love summer rain. Other people's failures make me sadder than my own. I do not rejoice in my enemies' failures. I have trouble understanding why people give stupid presents. Presents make me feel awkward, whether I am the giver or the receiver, unless they are the right ones, which is rare. Love has given me great pleasure but takes up too much time. As the surgeon's scalpel reveals my organs, love introduces other versions of myself, whose obscene novelty disgusts me. I am not ill. I go to the doctor no more than once a year. I am nearsighted and slightly astigmatic. I have never kissed a lover in front of my parents. In Corsica some friends took me to a beginners' class in underwater diving, a teacher led me down six meters in a few seconds, my left ear popped, back on the surface I had lost my sense of balance, since then whenever I'm in an airplane I feel a needle pricking my inner ear until, all at once, the air rushes out of my ear drum. I do not know the names of flowers. I recognize the chestnut tree, the lime tree, the poplar, the willow, the weeping willow, the oak, the chestnut, the pine, the fir, the beech, the sycamore, the hazelnut, the apple, the cherry, the lilac, the plum, the pear, the fig, the cedar, the sequoia, the baobab, the palm tree, the coconut, the live oak, the maple, the olive. I can name, but do not recognize, the ash, the aspen, the spindle tree, the strawberry tree, the bougainvillea, the catalpa. I have kept guppies, Sumatran brill, neons, a fish striped yellow and black and shaped like a snake, and other aquarium fish whose names I have forgotten. I had a female hamster called Pirouette because she loved her turquoise plastic wheel and ran so fast in it that it would spin her all the way round. A woman friend whose English isn't good heard *C'est quelque chose* for "Set in your shoes" in the song "Let's Groove." At times I have run down dark paths. An uncle would play Scorlipochon One Two Three Four Five Six Seven Eight Nine Ten with me, I had to say Scorlipochon one two three four five six seven eight nine ten while he was tickling me. One of my uncles had a taste for scandal and pranks, he'd shoplift just for fun, he would buy *Hara-Kiri* magazine and let me read it, he would pretend to be retarded at the beach, he would pounce yelling and drooling on a sunbathing woman, he'd ask questions using nonexistent words of the farmer's wife who lived down the road, he would call strangers on the phone and pretend they had a snake waiting to be picked up at Orly Airport, he went to the casino until he was definitively and cheerfully banned, he tried to win back the leases of nightclubs that his father had won at poker and he ended up getting drunk when the mafioso landlords plied him with champagne. I wonder how I would behave under torture. At a museum I look at people with the eyes of an artist, in the street with my own. I know four names for God. A friend told me that to yawn four times was the equivalent of fifteen minutes' sleep, I've often tried this without noting any benefits. I have known climates that went from twenty-five below to over forty-five degrees Celsius. I have met Catholics, Protestants, Mormons, Jews, Muslims, Hindus, Buddhists, Amish, Jehovah's Witnesses, Scientologists. I have seen earth, mountains, and sea. I have seen lakes, rivers, creeks, brooks, torrents, waterfalls. I have seen volcanoes. I have seen estuaries, coasts, islands, continents. I have seen caves, canyons, fairy hats. I have seen deserts, beaches, dunes. I have seen the sun and the moon. I have seen stars, comets, an eclipse. I have seen the Milky Way. I am no longer ten years old. I have never believed that you could see a dahu. I wonder if there are blasphemers of Satan, and if to blaspheme against him is a sin, from his point of view but also from God's. Monsters interest me. When I see the words "code PIN OK" on French bank machines, I read it as "code Pinoquet." Solitude helps me be consistent. A friend of my parents was fifty before she learned that there is no such thing as elbow grease. I did not know how to answer when a grown-up asked, "Is that lie really true?" I forced myself to smile when a grown-up said, "Go see if I'm over there." My father is funny. My mother loves me without smothering me. I discovered "dirty pictures" in a little blue pamphlet which described certain sins and which a priest had given me before my first confession to help me remember the ones I might have committed. I attended a school that employed several pedophiles, but I was not among their victims. One of my schoolmates, at age twelve, was followed by an old man into a stairwell, where he dragged him into a basement to have his way with him. The dog belonging to a friend of mine disfigured his best friend when my friend was fourteen. I have never missed a flight that then exploded in mid-air. I almost killed three passengers in my car by looking for a cassette in the glove compartment while I was going one-eighty on the highway from Paris to Reims.

My father walked in on me making love to a woman, when he knocked I said without thinking, "Come in," blushing, he quickly backed out and closed the door, when my girlfriend tried to slip away, he went up to her and said, "Come back whenever you like, mademoiselle." Like most people, I have no idea where the city I live in got its name. One of my uncles died of AIDS soon after the art gallery in which he'd invested all his money went out of business. One of my uncles met the love of his life while driving his red convertible slowly through the streets of Paris, the man in question, a Hungarian immigrant, was in despair, wandering aimlessly and about to kill himself, my uncle pulled up next to him and asked where he was headed, they never parted until death came between them. My uncle's friend taught me to laugh at things I saw on TV that were not, on the face of it, funny, for example Bobby Ewing's hairstyle on *Dallas*. I have not signed a manifesto. If I turn around while looking in the mirror, there comes a moment when I no longer see myself. Raymond Poulidor is one of the least sexy names I know. I like salad mainly for the crunch and the vinaigrette. I do not like to hear people quote bons mots, especially those of Sacha Guitry. I delight in the wrapping paper before acceding to the object. Visiting churches bores me, I wonder whether, apart from a few specialists, anybody enjoys it very much. I do not know the names of the stars. I often plan to learn long texts by heart in order to boost my memory. I see fantastical beings in the clouds. I have never seen a geyser, an atoll, an undersea trench. I have never done time in prison. I like dim lights. I have never filed a complaint with the police. I have never been burgled. When I was twelve, I took the metro with three classmates, a stranger my age bent my arm behind my back, another about fifteen years old kicked me in the face, I fell down, when I got up he was about to give me another kick, so I pretended to be in more pain than I was, grabbing my face with both hands and screaming as if he'd smashed it in, the attackers got scared and ran away, at which point my three "friends," who'd been standing there three meters away, ran up to me, I noticed the face of one had gone white with cowardice. My parents do not ask me enough questions. I once went into a prison where I was taking pictures of the inmates, in Rome, New York, a guard stopped me, he took me to the assistant warden, my film was confiscated, it also included photos of Jehovah's Witnesses taken in Paris, New York. I have sold works to collectors from France, Austria, Spain, Germany, Italy, America, and possibly other countries. If over time a woman I'm seeing starts to use the expressions I do, I may begin to pity her. I wish there were regions where every day was the same day of the week, I could decide to go spend five Mondays in one city and eight Saturdays in another. I wish there was a city where everyone was named Jean or Jeanne, it would be called Jeanville. Names draw me to places, but bodies draw me to people. I forget that certain names of objects refer to actions, for example "watch." I wonder whether anyone besides old people like riot police. I fetishize handwriting. When I choose postcards from a place, I am tempted to vary the pictures, rather than picking several with the best picture, which is absurd, since they're all going to different addressees. When I write several postcards on the same day, I force myself not to describe the same events, as if the addressees might one day realize that I had written the same postcard several times over. I have taken a ride through the ravines of the Golden Triangle on the back of a blind elephant who found his way by feeling around with his feet. My brother builds. I mistakenly studied difficult subjects that were no use to me when I might have studied the arts for pleasure, which would have smoothed my path. I am happy to be happy, I am sad to be sad, but I can also be happy to be sad and sad to be happy. Lack of sleep bothers me less on a sunny day than when it rains. I find someone beautiful regardless of the moment, but I don't always find myself handsome, therefore I am not. I sometimes talk to my dick, addressing it by its first name. I appreciate the mowed-hay smell of Levi's 501s. I do not tell stories because I forget the people's names, I report the events out of order and do not set up the punch line. On trips I surprise myself, for example I decide at a moment I did not expect that the trip is over. With a Dictaphone I write easily while thinking of something else. I have written several love letters but no breakup letters, I saved that job for my voice. I would rather paint chewing gum up close than Versailles from far away. I touch white for luck. I do not have a weekend place because I don't like to open and then close a whole lot of shutters over the course of two days. I would pay someone to air out, heat, and clean a country house before I came to stay, so I could have the feeling that someone lived there. Although I am self-employed, I observe the weekend. My surname is ridiculous, but I am fond of it, I even teach it to people who don't know it. I pack my luggage by making a list of all the things I will take, and since I always take the same things I keep the list in a file on my computer. I reuse grocery bags as trash bags. I separate my recycling, more or less. Drinking puts me to sleep. In Hong Kong I knew someone who went out three nights a week, no more, no less. I believe that democracy is spreading in the world. The modern man I sing. I feel better lying down than standing up and better standing than seated. I admire the person who thought up the title *The Last House on the Left*. A friend told me about the "Red Man of the Tuileries," I don't remember what he did but the name still gives me shivers. The pediatrician my mother took me to humiliated generations of children, including me, with this riddle: "If Vincent leaves a donkey in one meadow and goes into another meadow, how many donkeys are there?" all said in a measured voice, and then he'd say, "There's only one donkey—you" to any child, that is, every child, who didn't answer "One." I want to write sentences that begin "Ultimately." I can understand "It's the end," "It's the beginning of the end," "It's the beginning of the end of the beginning," but once we get to "It's the beginning of the end of the beginning of the end of the beginning," all I hear is a bunch of words. I have sometimes annoyed an interlocutor by systematically repeating the last word he said. I never get tired of saying *La fifille à son pépère* (grandfather's darling). One of my friends earns the admiration of some and the indifference of others by knowing the name and number of every département in France. My cousin Véronique is amazing. I sometimes think of the witty thing to say an hour later. At the table, I excused myself for splashing food on the spotless shirt of a friend by telling him: "You got in the way of my juice." I take no pleasure in others' misfortunes. I do not bow down before a metal idol. I am not horrified by my heritage. I do not till the earth. I do not expect to discover new marvels in classical music, but I'm sure of taking pleasure until I die in the ones I already know. I do not know whether one can improve on the music of Bach, but one can certainly improve on the music of several others who shall remain nameless. I admit to being wrong. I do not fight. I have never punched anyone. I have noticed that, on the keypads of Parisian front doors, the 1 wears out the fastest. I have sometimes turned my interlocutors against me by an excess of argumentation. I do not listen to jazz, I listen to Thelonious Monk, John Coltrane, Chet Baker, Billie Holiday. I sometimes feel like an impostor without knowing why, as if a shadow falls over me and I can't make it go away. If I travel with someone, I see half as much of the country as if I traveled by myself. One of my friends likes to travel in certain Middle Eastern countries where there is nothing to see but airports, deserts, and roads. I have never regretted traveling by myself, but I have sometimes regretted traveling with someone else. I read the Bible out of order. I do not read Faulkner, because of the translation. I made a series of pictures based on things that came out of my body or grew on it: whiskers, hair, nails, semen, urine, shit, saliva, mucus, tears, sweat, pus, blood. TV interests me more without the sound. Among friends I can laugh hard at certain unfunny TV programs that depress me when I'm alone. I never quite hear what people say who bore me. To me a simple "No" is pleasantly brief and upsettingly harsh. The noise level when it's turned up too high in a restaurant ruins my meal. If I had to emigrate I would choose Italy or America, but I don't. When I'm in a foreign country, I dream of having a house in Provence, a project I forget when I get back. I rarely regret a decision and always regret not having made one. I think back on the pain of affairs that never took place. The highway bores me, there's no life on the side of the road. On the highway the view is too far away for my imagination to bring it to life. I do not see what I lack. I have less desire to change things than to change my perception of them. I take pictures because I have no real desire to change things. I have no desire to change things because I am the youngest in my family. I like meeting new people when I travel: these brief and inconsequential encounters have the thrill of beginnings and the sadness of separations. I wanted to write a book entitled *In the Car,* made up of remarks recorded while driving. To take pictures at random goes against my nature, but since I like doing things that go against my nature, I have had to make up excuses to take pictures at random, for example, to spend three months in the United States traveling only to cities that share a name with a city in another country: Berlin, Florence, Oxford, Canton, Jericho, Stockholm, Rio, Delhi, Amsterdam, Paris, Rome, Mexico, Syracuse, Lima, Versailles, Calcutta, Baghdad. When I decide to take a picture of someone I see in the street, I have ten seconds to notice the person, decide to take the picture, and go ask, if I wait it's too late. I wear glasses. In my mouth, time moves slowly for candy. I have deeper to dig in myself. I see art where others see things. Between the solitude of the womb and the solitude of the tomb I will have hung out with lots of people. While driving a car past some meadows these words came to me: a tractor chicken and an elephant tent. I wish treatises were article- not book-length. In the United States I came across a village called Seneca Falls, which I mistranslated *Les Chutes de Seneque* (Seneca's Falls). I have seen an ad for a vegetarian vehicle. I would like to see movies accompanied by inappropriate music, a comedy with goth rock, a children's movie with music from a funeral, a romance with a brass band, a political film with a musical-comedy sound track, a war movie with acid rock, porn with a choir. I make fewer and fewer excuses. After I lick an envelope I spit. I don't want to die suddenly but to see death slowly coming. I do not think I will end up in hell. It takes five minutes for my nose to forget a smell, even a very bad one, this doesn't go for what I perceive with my other senses. I have weapons in my brain. I have read this sentence by Kerouac: "The war must have been getting in my bones." Although I have always translated *Deer Hunter* as *Chasseur de cerf*, I still hear the echo of the mistranslation *cher chasseur* (dear hunter). I remember what people tell me better than what I said. I expect to die at the age of eighty-five. To drive at night through rolling hills by moonlight in summertime can make me shudder with pleasure. I look more closely at old photographs than contemporary ones, they are smaller, and their details are more precise. If not for religion and sex, I could live like a monk. My last and first names mean nothing to me. If I look in the mirror for long enough, a moment comes when my face stops meaning anything. I can stand around in several dozen different ways. I have carried women in my arms, I have not been carried by them. I have not hugged a male friend tight. I have not walked hand in hand with a male friend. I have not worn a friend's clothing. I have not seen the dead body of a friend. I have seen the dead bodies of my grandmother and my uncle. I have not kissed a boy. I used to have sex with women my own age, but as I got older they got younger. I do not buy used shoes. I had an idea for an Amish punk band. Only once was I the first occupant of an apartment. I got into a motorcycle accident that could have cost me my life, but I don't have any bad memories of it. The present interests me more than the past, and less than the future. I have nothing to confess. I have trouble believing that France will go to war in my lifetime. I like to say thank you. I cannot perceive the delay in mirrors. I don't like narrative movies any more than I like the novel. "I do not like the novel" doesn't mean I do not like literature, "I don't like narrative movies" doesn't mean I don't like movies. Art that unfolds over time gives me less pleasure than art that stops it. The second time I walk the same route, I pay less attention to the view and walk faster. I let the phone ring until the answering machine screens the call. I spend two hours talking to one friend, but it only takes five minutes to end my conversation with another. When I'm on the phone, I don't make any effort with my face. If I put off a phone call where something is at stake, the wait becomes more difficult than the call. I am impatient when waiting for a phone call but not when I have to make one. I have more good memories than bad ones. When I'm sure I like an article of clothing I buy a few of the same one. I do not wish to shine. At sixteen I bought a varsity jacket, it was aquamarine with beige leather sleeves, I only wore it twice, I felt, wrongly, that everyone was looking at me. I have read *The Critique of Judgment*. I used to make the stretchers for the canvases I painted. I have let several friends copy from me in class. When I was thirteen, in the Galeries Lafayette, I stole several records, I put them under my arm, I strolled nonchalantly down the lingerie aisle where I slipped them into my bag, as I left the store someone grabbed my scarf from behind, I turned around, it was a fifty-year-old security guard, she took me into a fluorescent-lit office, she threatened to call the police, I made myself cry, I said my parents were unemployed and about to get a divorce, which was untrue, she let me go, she seemed embarrassed, almost guilty, since then I have stolen books once and once some paperclips, without really knowing why. I get excited by the idea of reading the biography of an author I love, then when I actually do it I lose steam. I have read only four biographies all the way through: *Raymond Roussel*, by François Caradec, *Blue Monk*, by Jacques Ponzio and François Postif, *La Vie douloureuse de Charles Baudelaire*, by François Porché, and *Kerouac: A Biography*, by Ann Charters. I spend a lot of time reading, but I do not consider myself a "big reader." I reread. On my shelves I count as many books read as unfinished. Counting up the books I have read, I cheat by counting the ones I didn't finish. I will never know how many books I have read. Raymond Roussel, Charles

Baudelaire, Marcel Proust, Alain Robbe-Grillet, Antonio Tabucchi, André Breton, Olivier Cadiot, Jorge Luis Borges, Andy Warhol, Gertrude Stein, Ghérasim Luca, Georges Perec, Jacques Roubaud, Joe Brainard, Roberto Juarroz, Guy Debord, Fernando Pessoa, Jack Kerouac, La Rochefoucauld, Baltasar Gracian, Roland Barthes, Walt Whitman, Nathalie Quintane, the Bible, and Bret Easton Ellis all matter to me. I have read less of the Bible than of Marcel Proust. I prefer Nathalie Quintane to Baltasar Gracian. Guy Debord matters more to me than Roland Barthes. Roberto Juarroz makes me laugh more than Andy Warhol. Jack Kerouac makes me want to live more than Charles Baudelaire. La Rochefoucauld depresses me less than Bret Easton Ellis. Olivier Cadiot cheers me up more than André Breton. Joe Brainard is less affirmative than Walt Whitman. Raymond Roussel surprises me more than Baltasar Gracian, but Baltasar Gracian makes me more intelligent. Gertrude Stein writes texts more nonsensical than those of Jorge Luis Borges. I read Bret Easton Ellis more easily on the train than Raymond Roussel. I know Jacques Roubaud less well than Georges Perec. Ghérasim Luca is the most full of despair. I don't see the connection between Alain Robbe-Grillet and

Antonio Tabucchi. When I make lists of names, I dread the ones I forget. I read for half an hour before I turn out the light. I read more in the morning and evening than in the afternoon. I do not use glasses for reading. I read from thirty centimeters away. I start to really read after minute five. I read better without shoes or pants. Nights with a full moon I feel euphoric for no reason. I do not read at the beach. At the beach I start off bored, then I get used to it, then I hate to leave. At the beach girls arouse me less than in the library. I like museums, mainly because they tire me out. I make no predictions. I like, in order of preference, swimming in the sea, in a lake, in a creek, in a pool. I have swum in the canyon of Gardon, near Collias, flat smooth rocks line the stream that flows softly at a pleasant temperature, I climbed over three hundred meters to its source and came back without the slightest effort, as in a dream, the sun cast an orange sheen on the surface of the rocks, my eyes could see far into the distance and my words echoed. I don't think about going to the movies. I have made love standing on the roof of the chateau de Tarascon during the opening of a show of André-Pierre Arnal. I have made love on the roof of the thirtieth floor of a building in Hong Kong. I have made love in the daytime in a public garden in Hong Kong. I have made love in the toilet of the Paris-Lyon TGV. I have made love in front of some friends at the end of a very drunken dinner. I have made love in a staircase on the avenue Georges-Mandel. I have made love to a girl at a party at six in the morning, five minutes after asking, without any preamble, if she wanted to. I have made love standing up, sitting down, lying down, on my knees, stretched out on one side or the other. I have made love to one person at a time, to two, to three, to more. I have smoked hashish and opium, I have done poppers, I have snorted cocaine. I find fresh air more intoxicating than drugs. I smoked my first joint at age fourteen in Segovia, a friend and I had bought some "chocolate" from a guard in the military police, I couldn't stop laughing and I ate the leaves of an olive tree. I smoked several joints on the grounds of my Catholic grammar school, le collège Stanislas, at the age of fifteen. At seventeen in Paris I drove my parents' car without a license to take the girl home who had just spent part of the night with me. The girl whom I loved the most left me. I wear black shirts. At ten I cut my finger in a flour mill. At six I broke my nose getting hit by a car. At fifteen I skinned my hip and elbow by falling off a moped, I thought I would defy the street, riding with no hands, looking backward. I broke my thumb skiing, after flying ten meters and landing on my head, I got up and saw, as in a cartoon, circles of birthday candles turning in the air, and then I fainted. I have not made love to the wife of a friend. On the Internet I become telepathic. I do not love the sound of a family on the train. I am uneasy in rooms with small windows. I wonder how the obese make love. I feel good the moment I reach the top of a skyscraper. I could not live on a ground floor or in a basement. The higher the floor number, the better I feel. Sometimes I realize that what I'm in the middle of saying is boring, so I just stop talking. I used to think I worked better at night than in daytime until one day I bought black curtains. I use the shell of the first mussel to spoon out the rest. I can do without TV. I love saying *pupull* instead of *pull*. I don't know which disturbs me more, an actor who goes into politics, Ronald Reagan, or a politician who takes up acting, Bernard Tapie. I had an idea for a gallery-hanging that would begin four days after the opening, during which the people who came would have their pictures taken, and be the subject of the exhibition. When I've slept badly, my breathing is shallow. I believe the people who make the world are the ones who do not believe in reality, for example, for centuries, the Christians. Not wanting to change things doesn't mean I am conservative, I like for things to change, just not having to be the one who does it. I can't tell whether my fantasies match my capacities. I have spent two summers in a red van. Virtuosity annoys me, it confuses art with prowess. I have thought simultaneously: "I really should learn the trombone" and "there's a dead ant." If I get up early the day feels longer than if I get up late, even if I spend the same amount of time awake. Smoking takes too long. Drinking helps me sleep but keeps me from sleeping through the night. Drinking gives me a headache the morning after. I prefer movies with costumes from the future to ones with costumes from the past. My ideas are more my style than my words are. In a car I look at things through the windshield as if they were in a tracking shot. Maybe I'm writing this book so I won't have to talk anymore. I've bought an apartment from a smiling crook. I do not explain. I do not excuse. I do not classify. I go fast. I do not name the people I talk about to someone who doesn't know them, I use, despite the trouble of it, abstract descriptions like "that friend whose parachute got tangled up with another parachute the time he jumped." In the morning I spend half an hour lying in the dark before the alarm goes off. I prefer going to bed to getting up, but I prefer living to dying. I do not respond to unpleasant remarks, but I do not forget them. Certain people wear me out in seconds because I can tell they are going to bore me. In Versailles, New York, I photographed a seventy-five-year-old man who wore black glasses, a cap, a stained white T-shirt under a Dickies-brand chambray shirt with the sleeves rolled up, beat up jeans, and black work boots, he was sad and handsome, I found out his name was Edward Lee, almost like mine. Driving once I thought I saw a road sign that said "Cheese Clinic," I wondered whether they took care of cheese there or of people, using cheese. On the road I can be boxed in, or tailed, by the shadows of clouds. I watch the asphalt markings disappear under the hood of the car like strings of licorice. I find thin people make me feel young. Contemporary music generally seems aggressive to me, not because it's contemporary but because it's full of aggression. Certain non-aggressive music by Ligeti, Cage, Messiaen, Lutoslawski, Penderecki, Adams agrees with me. I like conversations you can interrupt without being rude: phone conversations, conversations with neighbors over the fence, conversations with the regulars at bistros, conversations with strangers. My grandmother was introduced to my grandfather because they both liked gusts of wind. One of my uncles answered an advertisement placed by a South African planter, seeking an orange-grower, as follows: "I know nothing about agriculture but am a quick study" and got the job. In South Africa one of my aunts had a servant named Coca-Cola and another named Shell. In the mornings one of my cousins and I used to play squirrels in a big bed, we'd hide under the covers, he would say "A touino touine, touine, touine, touine, a touino touine, touinoldin," and cluck his tongue. In la Creuse one of my cousins and I used to play farmer and little lamb, the lamb would roll around in his underpants in a trough made out of a mud puddle, the farmer would watch him and play around vaguely with a stick, mostly he was the lamb, I was the farmer. In Corsica I used to play "girlwatcher." In Normandy I used to play with Action Men. I have changed at least one tire. I have had a white R5, a gray Fiat Uno, a gray BMW 316, a gray Volkswagen Polo Movie, a red Volkswagen Transporter. When I ride a motorcycle I wear a thick black leather

Vanson jacket, even in summer. In Paris I ride a bike. I do not fall down in roller skates. I have a double chin. I do not wear black socks with shorts. I do not wear a wool sweater if my neck is damp. I will sign up for a paragliding course. I forget to watch TV. I do not have a favorite tree, a favorite singer, a favorite friend, a favorite pair of pants, a favorite dessert. I wear the clothes of a manual laborer. If I lean off a balcony with the desire to kill myself, vertigo saves me. I like watching anything shot on Super 8, even though this is in such predictable good taste. I have no inclinations toward pedophilia. Urine does not excite me, neither do dogs. I breathe well with my mouth open. If it didn't make me look stupid I would keep my mouth open a lot of the time. Aviation does not interest me. My brother thought his turtle had run away, it dried up under a radiator. I have trouble remembering any truly happy moments. I would like to have myself hypnotized by my wife, but I'm not married. Contradicting myself brings two kinds of pleasure: betraying myself and having a new opinion. I do things better for pleasure and without trying. When I urinate in a public toilet I breathe through my mouth, not my nose, even though it's closer than my nostrils to the source of the smell. At a public urinal the presence of a neighbor delays my micturition. Into the sitting room of my parents' country house walked my godmother, her three children, and the girlfriend of one of her sons, whose beauty so overwhelmed me that I forgot to say hello to my godmother, and when she pointed out the omission, I walked over and shook her hand instead of giving her a kiss. I love the crackle of a parquet floor. I have flat feet. The cold of floorboards travels through my bare feet up to my shins, which get goose bumps. I can take seafood or leave it. Everything interests me a priori, but not a posteriori. I do not think the dead are malevolent, since they are old people squared, and the old are less malevolent than the non-old. Virtuosity also bores me when it comes to roads: the highway is perfect and perfectly boring. If, driving fast, I don't use windshield wipers, the size of the raindrops shrinks by evaporation. I could found an imprint for perversely themed guidebooks on the following subjects: McMansions, dangerous traffic lights, so-called museums, places where there's nothing much to see, places where an archbishop may have slept. Driving alone over a bridge mounted with sky-blue rails I cried out with pointless joy and shouted nonsensical words. Listening to cheerful music is like spending time with people not like me. I have never attended a nudist funeral. I accept progress. I desire an object less if it was bought on sale. I am wary of shortcuts, which call the normal route into question. A hand that greets me by crushing my hand bodes no better than a hand that is soft or moist. When I laugh I use fewer facial muscles than when I don't, to rest my face I have to laugh. In a car, perfume makes me sick. When I am hungry I feel thin. I liked Jimmy Carter. I wonder whether I admire faith or just people who have it. On the highway if several cars are speeding, I follow them to divide up the risk of getting stopped. I have left a woman because she scolded me for not having picked up groceries. In a foreign country the words missing from my pocket dictionary acquire an aura that doesn't fade when I learn their ostensible meanings. I am more excited by a woman's face than by her breasts than by her pussy than by her ass than by her legs. Obesity fascinates me because it effaces sex and age. I stand up straighter when I walk with a knapsack than when I don't. My torso is too long for me to be comfortable in a car. I am afraid of doing worse by trying to do better. The dry look is an inexhaustible source of amusement, even when I'm alone.

I have a feeling children of my own would bore me less than other people's. I do not sleep on satin sheets. I wonder how I can just suddenly come out with: "Oh la la!" The problem with amusement parks is the crowds: empty I find them beautiful. I have smoked so much I felt sick. I am able to admire people who admire me. I do not embellish things or make them ugly either. I like serial music until the moment when, suddenly, I can't stand it. Listening to music in the car is a way of passing the time, thus shortening my life. My cars have always drifted to the right. Bad news makes me unhappy but satisfies my paranoia. I can see a lot of my body. My mother saved my life by giving me life. When I have finished with a thing I don't throw it down, I put it down. A Louis-Philippe tart makes me hungrier than a bouillabaisse which costs more than a quartz watch which is more use than a book of jokes which makes me laugh less than my cousin Cyrille. I do not love the accordion, but I love the bandoneón. I prefer the cello to the violin. I am a meticulous packer. I go months without reading the paper. I make regular trips to galleries. I can't handle too much art at once. I do not enjoy contemporary art fairs. I leave an art fair the way I leave a book fair: disabused. I have too great a sense of the absurd to do the accent when I speak a foreign language. To make it through the afternoon I turn it into a cold night: blinds closed, curtains drawn. I write in bed. In a pool by the side of the road, I have turned the sound of the cars into waves. It seems I do not snore. Having goose bumps reminds me that I was an animal, generations ago. I will not lose my eyesight, I will not lose my hearing, I will not wet myself, I will not forget who I am, I will die first. I wipe the table before and after eating. I do not remember having been punished by my parents. I taught myself to type. I taught myself everything I know about computers. I enjoy playing anything on the piano as long as no one is listening. I do not say "Double or nothing," "I dare you," or "A bird in the hand is worth two in the bush." For several years I wore Pour Monsieur by Chanel, then White by Comme des Garcons, then Philosykos by Diptyque. I am against stucco. I do not like exposed stone any better than exposed beams. In company, I am less guilty when I transgress. I have not predicted that Mick Jagger will die of prostate cancer. I have a weakness for negative formulations, counter-formulations, reformulations, and deformations. When I expect to achieve nothing, ideas come. When I hear the English word "god," I think both of God and of a dildo (*godemi-ché*). When I want to make a friend laugh, I say apropos of nothing: "How immoral." During a comic movie, the anticipatory laughter of the other viewers leaves me unable to laugh. At a dinner party, a girlfriend kissed me, took off her clothes, and ruined everything for half the guests, including three old lovers of mine. Playing ping-pong, the sound of the ball helps me more than its color. I like living in a house that is freighted with the pasts of other people, I also like sleeping in anonymous hotels. I have left a woman because I didn't love her anymore and didn't like the way I was around her. I feel apprehensive before conversations that have a fixed duration: lunches, dinners, interviews. With more than six people at the table, I get lost in all the conversation. I prefer conversations for two. I would rather have dinner with one person than with several. Swimming is like a kind of sleep: I go easily from a bed to a lake. If I swim for half an hour in the morning, I feel good all day. When I relax completely in a pool, I always end up in the same position, back to the sky, body bent at forty-five degrees, head underwater, arms stretched out in front as if to grab the void. I have never gone to a strip club. I have gone to bed with roughly fifteen prostitutes, of various extractions: French, Indian, African, Romanian, Arab, Italian, Albanian. Louis de Funès depresses me. I have a collection of about twenty pairs of blue jeans. I have a collection of pairs of black leather oxfords. I have a collection of black shirts. I have a collection of black leather jackets. I have a collection of black socks. I have a collection of black underpants. I have a collection of jean jackets. People who don't know me well think I am always wearing the same shirt and jeans. I have never considered sleeping with a nun. When a machine stops humming is when I notice it's been getting on my nerves. I am not planning to take revenge. I always keep a tissue in one pocket and keys in the other. I'm not sure I can be psychoanalyzed. Buying clothes is a trial, wearing them a pleasure. I am in favor of same-sex marriage. I like doing things twice but the third time makes me sad. I sniff the book I'm reading. I sneeze three times in a row. I do not take out my dick in public. I look at the real estate ads in windows without any intention of buying. When I look out a window, I also look at the reflections. I would rather look at objects behind glass than on a shelf. I would rather look at a piece of clothing folded on a shelf than hanging on a rack. I press my finger against soft putty. Bruno Gibert and Cyril Casmèze are the people who make me laugh the most. I do not chew chewing gum. I am as taken with new clothes as with a new identity. I regret not having been a radical in my youth. I could become politically engaged in the cause of an environmentalist party. When I was young, Nazism seemed to belong to another era, but the older I get the closer this era seems to be. I have trouble explaining why we have five digits. After too long in the bath my fingers wrinkle up. I perceive only my bones that ache. My favorite composers are Bach and Debussy. I do not whistle while I work. When I whistle, I become winded. Hearing someone whistle annoys me, especially with vibrato. I feel uneasy hearing someone sing a capella while looking me in the eyes, which luckily happens only on TV. I don't know what to say to test an echo so I say "Oooooh." To me, air conditioned air seems perfumed with dust and microbes. I feel no nostalgia for my childhood, my youth, or what came next. I am tempted to make exhaustive lists, and stop myself in the middle. I am not lyrical. I like to travel in order to stop in another place. Life seems interminable to me like a Sunday afternoon to a child. Thursday is the best night. There is no "best" week. I have no memories of being hurt by women, only by men. When she is bored, one of my friends gets dressed and made up as if she were going out, and doesn't. When he is in a foreign country, one of my friends follows nice-looking strangers in the street to find a party. I say everything. I have never made much money, but this hasn't bothered me. I own my apartment. I may prefer one of my parents to the other, but I would rather not think about it. I can do without music, art, architecture, dance, theater, movies, I have trouble doing without photography, I cannot do without literature. Digging a hole makes me feel good. The sound of water bothers me. I have few regrets. I do not seek novelty, but rightness. I wept reading *Perfecto*, by Thierry Fourreau. All of the music by Daniel Darc, The Durutti Column, Portishead, The Doors, and Dominique A agrees with me. I have a fantasy of eavesdropping on what gets said in the office of a notary for a week. I do not have the fantasy of doing the same in an analyst's office. For the sake of taking a walk, I park my motorcycle at some distance from a rendezvous. When I'm abroad, everything is more or less unreal, which sometimes makes me want to live there, except I would still have to change countries since it would no longer be "abroad." I regret having spoken but not having kept quiet. I make lots of little works instead of undertaking a big one. I do not wear T-shirts with images or text. I feel good if I work well, but I can work well without feeling good. I can't get no satisfaction. Walking helps me get ready to work. When I walk I have no ideas, I get ready to have some when I sit down. I made myself laugh out loud with an idea for a book to be entitled: *My Conspiracy Theories*. I think Carine Charaire is right to be so utterly herself. I have sixty pairs of pants, forty shirts, eighteen jackets or sport coats, and twenty-five pairs of socks, which makes one million eighty thousand outfits. I do not like whimsy (*fantaisie*) or the word *fantaisie*. I am hostile to the concept of the aperitif. One of my friends does not like women who like men. I use the word "girls" for women I find attractive regardless of age. When I am tired, I feel physically unwell in my feet, in my lower and upper back, at the back of my neck, and in my temples. I don't mind the cold. I am unacquainted with hunger. I was never in the army. I have never pulled a knife on anyone. I have never used a machine gun. I have fired a revolver. I have fired a rifle. I have shot an arrow. I have netted butterflies. I have observed rabbits. I have eaten pheasants. I recognize the scent of a tiger. I have touched the dry head of a tortoise and an elephant's hard skin. I have caught sight of a herd of wild boar in a forest in Normandy. I ride. I do not always find beautiful women exciting, or the women who excite me beautiful. I rest only against my will. I have no guide and am a guide to no one. I help myself at the table until there's nothing left. At border crossings I feel as good as if I were nowhere. I sleep in the middle of the bed. I think of objects in terms of their edges. I use soft bags more often than hard suitcases. I would rather live in a port town. I do not have fantasies of living on a desert island. Removing a splinter brings a sharp pleasure. When I remove a Band-Aid I get excited at the moment of truth: will the scab come off? The faster I remove a Band-Aid, the less it pulls my hair. I encounter very little opposition. I wish I smiled less. I hope some day my friends might come and sit under my vine and my fig tree. I am pitiless toward the wicked. I am against the death penalty. I am surprised there is no word for a mistaken sense of déjà vu. I have been locked in a cellar. I was not beaten. I was not insulted. No one abused me. I sometimes read things back to front. I will never be done with literature. I do not use idiomatic expressions. I do not do public impressions. I ought to invent calisthenics to do in bed. I hope to be buried in a crypt of my own in Montparnasse. I hope to ask an aide to the Minister of Culture to construct my future crypt as a work of art, bearing my date of birth and a projected date of death, December 31, 2050. I no longer remember the exact number of countries on Earth, I think there are a few more than two hundred. I sharpen knives. I wash the dishes. I clear the table. I vacuum. I do windows. I scrub enameled surfaces. My ideal temperatures are twenty degrees outside, twenty-four inside. When it starts to rain, I smell things better. The hum of machinery puts me to sleep. When a machine stops humming it sometimes wakes me up. I've tried to rewrite my will when I wanted to kill myself, but I stopped myself partway through. I am a good listener. I do not think things were better before or will get better later on. One of my male friends has died. None of my female friends has died. Marc-Ernest Fourneau has seen me do what few men have seen me do. I have "sung" under the direction of Arnaud Labelle-Rojoux and Guy Scarpetta. I have designed the set for a runway show by Gaspard Yurkievich. I jump for joy but I do not sink down in sadness. I eschew unusual words. For me going back to a place after twenty years is stranger than smoking hashish. In public places music bothers me. I am drawn to the brevity of English, shorter than French. I had the idea for a book whose chapters would be anagrams of my name: *L'ode au verde, Rêve de l'ado U, Élève au Drod, Rue de Lovade, Ed roule Dave* (The Ode to Verde, Dream of Teen U, Pupil at the Drod, Rue de Lovade, Ed Rolls Dave). With my glasses off, if I stretch out my arms I can't make out my fingers. At the table, ice or bubbles make water less boring, but I like water boring. I have trouble believing men who say they have never gone to bed with a prostitute. Wine poisons me, cigarettes kill me, drugs bore me. I cannot name one hundredth of the components of my body. My nails grow for no reason. The pressure of the chair in summer on the skin of my back hurts in a nice way. To Joyce, who writes about banal things in extraordinary language, I prefer Raymond Roussel, who writes unrealistic things in everyday words. When I want to see theater, I go to Mass. I love the unpredictability of blue jeans: how, after you wash them, they shrink, age, fade. I am against reverence. When I was a child, I looked at rugs the same way, as a grown-up, I look at an abstract painting. When I was a child, the only group games I liked were ones that took place outdoors, without equipment, and without keeping score: tag and eeny meeny miney mo. I wasted time trying to be good at math. I am in favor of simplified spelling. I taught myself the things that mattered to me most: to write and to take pictures. Reasoning doesn't convince me, but it reassures me. I hope that at my death no religious ceremony will be observed. In my mouth what's hard turns soft and what's soft, liquid. I have fainted three times, during skiing or motorcycle accidents. I feel put off by a man who talks too close, and follows me when I back away. Putting two things together that are unrelated gives me an idea. Close to the ground my memories of childhood come back. I play squash and ping-pong. When I lie down after drinking water, my stomach makes noises like a water bed. I cross certain streets not breathing through my nose to avoid pollution. I am not for or against painting, that would be like being for or against the brush. When I am happy I'm afraid of dying, when I'm unhappy I am afraid of not dying. If I don't like what I see, I close my eyes, but if what I hear bothers me, I am unable to close my ears. I cannot predict my headaches. I empty my memory. Squeezing a sponge is fun like chewing gum. Sometimes I will spend the day thinking about a phrase that came to me out of nowhere and that I don't understand, such as: "The last time it was yesterday." If I think of it as a performance, packing a suitcase becomes a joy. I make modified recordings of Wagner where I keep only the parts that suit me, slow, sad, and without voices. I often have trouble sleeping. I stopped having nightmares during adolescence, or rather: I still dream about terrifying things, without being terrorized. I write less and less with a pen, more and more on a computer. I bought more records at twenty than I buy at forty. I have worn Levi's 501s since I was fourteen, I got the idea when I was ten at my grandmother's reading a comic strip about a cowboy, but I had to wait four years to find jeans like that. It was very hard for me to tell my mother that I loved her, it took me until I was thirty-five. My mother told me she loved me when I was thirty-nine, or else she told me before and I forgot. I told my father that I loved him when I was depressed, at thirty-five, I was thinking of killing myself, I thought it would be a shame to die without telling him. I haven't told my brother that I loved him. I did not tell my grandmother that I loved her. I have told five women that I loved them, which in four cases was true. I have sometimes made love to one woman while thinking of another.

I speak French fluently, I speak English well, I speak Spanish badly, I can vaguely understand a little bit of Italian. I learned Latin at school, what I remember is one declension. I see no point in holding on to my old toothbrushes. My favorite months are September and April, September for the resumption of social activity, April for the arrival of spring and the progressive denudification of women. I am not an expert in anything. I have subjects of conversation besides myself. I form very few hard and fast judgments about politics, the economy, and international affairs. I do not like bananas. International news, even dramatic news, leaves me pretty much indifferent, I feel guilty about that. I do not remember the first time I saw a character die in a movie or a book, but I remember the first time I saw a dead man, more precisely, I saw a man's leg sticking out of the trunk of a black car on the boulevard Berthier, I remember this detail: he was missing a shoe, and his sock was purple. My feet are always hot, sandals would help, but they're too ugly. I rarely wear hiking socks, they're too hot and make your feet stink. I would suggest that the authorities replace gun shops with swingers' clubs. The American accent both fascinates and repels me: the comedy of swallowed syllables, my fear of the dominant mode of speech. I prefer French as spoken by Italians to Italian as spoken by the French. I like to imitate the accent of a German of Vietnamese origins forcing himself to speak English. A Russian accent sends shivers down my spine. A Cantonese accent has less charm for me than an Indian accent. An Anglo-Indian accent inspires immediate sympathy in me. My mother stopped making family photo albums when I became an adolescent. I don't make photo albums. I take very few pictures of my friends. I have taken more pictures of myself than of my friends. I have almost realized a photo project that I described in Œuvres entitled *Facial Year*, in which I would take a photo of my face every day and make a film of the three hundred sixty-five images, I say "almost" since the film comprises two hundred photographs taken over a year and a half. I started a photo project in which I would photograph the forty-one places where Charles Baudelaire lived in Paris, but four years later I still hadn't finished, each time I think of going back to it, I'm discouraged by the idea that I would have to start at the beginning to make the pictures go together. One day I decided to classify the "unclassified" photographs I had taken over the last fifteen years, only to discover that they included at least ten categories, among them: friends, girlfriends, family, passersby, walls, shop windows, objects, windows, doors, I thought it would take me days to come up with these classifications, in three hours it was done. I stopped taking tourist photos when I realized that I looked at them only once, on the way back from the lab, just to confirm that they had no interest beyond what they were: travel pictures. When traveling I am always tempted, despite what I think of tourist photos, to take pictures of the beautiful land-scapes, the strangers in the streets, or the unlikely things I notice in store windows, I don't give in to this tempta-tion because I've gotten out of the habit of taking a cam-era with me on trips. I think tourists don't look at their travel photos, and if they do, think nothing of them. I could have been a journalist or reporter, a musician or a dancer. I can walk for hours without getting blisters on my feet. In a house I don't like green walls whether they're painted, hung with fabric, or wallpapered, green makes me think of a hospital or luxuriant vegetation, I don't want to be sick or in nature. There are times in my life when I overuse the phrase: "It all sounds pretty compli-cated." I have been to New York's Chinatown, I walked down Mott Street, Mulberry Street, Canal Street, and Bayard Street, all I saw were restaurants, shops selling gadgets, gifts, and jewelry, without being able to tell them apart I was stunned by the opacity of these few streets, I could penetrate them physically but not mentally, my mind hung back on the threshold, I saw nothing of Chinatown, but I bought a pair of black acrylic wool gloves for five dollars from an old Chinese man who was nervous. I need to stretch for at least fifteen minutes in the morning, otherwise my muscles are tense until evening, I work badly and am on edge. I rarely smoke more than ten cigarettes a day, my throat has a natural gauge that, if I smoke more, upsets my stomach. I have sometimes gone without smoking for days. I have stopped smoking several times by accident, always the same way: when I have a sore throat I stop smoking and, when it goes away, I forget to restart. I smoke roll-your-owns because they burn down at the same speed that I drag on them, if they go out, I relight them, manufactured cigarettes burn down on their own and impose a rhythm I don't want to follow. I have a friend who calculates that at three in the afternoon the metro is emptiest and so you always ought to take it exactly then. Sometimes I write on a computer with my eyes closed and look forward to the typos that will appear when I read it back. There is more about my body that I don't know than I know. I know I have a head, a right brain and a left brain, two eyes, two nostrils, teeth, a lower lip and an upper lip, I know I have ten fingers at the ends of my hands at the ends of my arms connected to my torso, a neck, two nipples, I forget how many ribs, a penis, two testicles, two buttocks, two hips, two legs and two feet, I know I have a stomach, a heart, a large intestine and a small one, a liver, a trachea, blood, a throat, a tongue, vocal chords, and two ears, I don't know how many muscles I have, how much my bones weigh, how many neurons I have or how quickly they are replenished, I don't know the volume of my blood, I have seen none of my internal organs, I have seen certain parts of my body only through the intermediary of a mirror, I have never seen certain parts of my body, even through the intermediary of a mirror, but I have no idea which. I follow madmen in the street. I am not an anarchist. I am not a communist. I am not a socialist. I am not on the Right. I am a democrat. Ecological issues matter to me. I have voted Green in every election. Until I was fourteen I spent most of my weekends in a country house where, looking back, I think I was very bored although I did not know it at the time. In poetry, I don't like the worked-over language, I like the facts and ideas. I am more interested in the neutrality and anonymity of our shared language than by the attempts of poets to make a language of their own, a factual report seems to me the most beautifully unpoetic poetry there is. I often use the word often. When I write I often use the word *beaucoup*, but on rereading I strike it. I dream of an objective prose, but there is no such thing. I don't know how many words I know. I wonder whether I forget words as I get older, and if, since I'm learning fewer words than I used to, the number of words I use is shrinking. I am often afraid of deceiving my interlocutors. I am uneasy speaking in public on subjects other than myself. I am inexhaustible on the subject of myself. Since I like listening to other people talk about themselves, I have no scruples about talking about myself. I ask lots of questions about my interlocutors' private lives, especially if we are strangers. I would rather have someone tell me about an exhibition than see it with my own eyes. I do not lie. I think I don't believe in God, but from time to time, at night, I wonder whether I ever really stopped believing. By my calculations, before the age of fourteen I believed in God by imitation, between fourteen and twenty-one I had faith, then more and more I stopped believing, until one day I realized I no longer believed. When I believed, I thought of God as a grandfather with a white tunic and beard, he appeared to me leaning down, as in a fresco. I dislike professional meetings where I show my work to people who see me out of politeness, not because they want to, I especially dislike the way they flip too quickly through my books of photos, as for professional meetings that go well, I don't always enjoy them, especially when they end in a commission that I only half believe in even though I pretend to be enthusiastic. When I'm sleeping well, I envision this project: to spend days without sleeping, to live with the feeling of being under the influence of a natural drug. When I'm sleeping badly, I envision this project: to sleep for forty-eight hours, to live afterward with the feeling of having been under the influence of a natural drug. In foreign countries eating presents a problem: the menus are incomprehensible, I choose at random and in general have had pleasant surprises although, or because, the nature of the dishes is unpredictable, and their order goes against nature. I am as deeply affected by good news as by bad, besides, bad news can be good, the real bad news would be no news at all. On the street I checked my watch while I was holding a can of Coke in my left hand, I poured part of it down my pants, by chance nobody saw, I have told no one. I have not read Plato, but I have read many articles that cited him, so I have the false sense of knowing him, like those books I've owned for a long time and never opened. To keep from being caught out, I avoid quoting Plato in the course of a conversation. I find it dangerous to invoke the views of a writer I know only partially, but there is none I know all the way through. A storm exalts me like an enemy. I can drink three big cups of American coffee without feeling sick, but no more than one French espresso and no Italian espresso at all. In foreign countries urinating and defecating is a problem, but no more so than when I'm away from home in my own country. I have not operated a truck, a plane, a helicopter, or a rocket, I drive cars, I ride motorcycles of all different cylinders, I pilot boats, I ride bicycles. I know how to downhill ski, water-ski, skateboard, roller-skate, wind-surf, but I don't know how to surf or snowboard. If I hear someone addressed as "Monsieur Paul" instead of "Paul" I have to overcome a sense of anxiety in order to keep talking to him, since I am making fun of him in my mind and will feel guilty afterward. I do not wear turtlenecks, they irritate my neck. I avoid Shetland sweaters because they itch and give off a smell that reminds me of the irritations I had as a child when I was forced to wear one. I do not like putting on a crewneck sweater when my hair is still damp. I stopped going to the hairdresser when I was fourteen because of the smell of the hair spray, the hard fingers of the shampoo woman on my wet hair, and the way my neck hurt on the U-shaped rim of the sink. I cut my own hair, which surprises my friends because with experience I tend not to get it wrong. I have seen too many grinning corpses on TV. I collect invitations to exhibitions so I can draw up an inventory in twenty or thirty years but every four years I throw them all away for lack of space, and, after a while, I start over again. I'd like to save all the postcards that I receive but I end up throwing them away after a few years, except the ones from my best friends. I wonder whether my friends throw away the postcards I worked so hard on before I sent them. I will repeat sentences or opinions that I've heard, verbatim, just because I think they're right and I don't see any reason to modify them before I take them as my own. I'm not sure that I can serve as a model for youth. When I was ten I was eating a ham sandwich, suddenly I caught a whiff of tobacco even though no one around me was smoking, along with this smell came a bitter taste in my mouth, there was a black cigarette butt in the baguette, I had just bitten into it. Unlike a friend of a friend, I have never found a tadpole in my yoghurt. On a winter day when no cloud darkens the sun and the cold light casts hard shadows, I could photograph anything and anyone. In public toilets, before I flush I wrap my fingers with toilet paper, I put paper down on the seat before I sit down, I wash my hands on the way out, but sometimes also on the way in. I have not found myself waiting for a train or plane that never arrived, only people. It's rare for me to make friends with someone who stands me up. I do not court a capricious woman. To reassure myself, when I am lost in a foreign city, I go to the supermarket, it's a familiar place, and yet, from close up, no product is similar to the ones I know, for example, I can be completely lost in the yoghurt aisle. I am attracted to women who are generous with their time, their smiles, their conversation, their affection, and their physical desire. I would rather be at the top of a mountain than at the bottom. I go down stairs one stair at a time and I climb them two by two. I have gone fishing fewer than five times, and not since I was fifteen. I shot a rifle at a pheasant, and I killed it. I shot a rifle at a blackbird, and I missed. I have torn the wings off roughly thirty flies, I have taken the back legs off a similar number of grasshoppers. I have crushed a hundred soldier ants on a lime tree in la Beauce. I have destroyed an anthill by kicking it. I deeply loved a dog that my parents had put down because he'd gone crazy, it was my first experience of death. I was sitting on a café terrace on a street near the Bastille, the bag with my expensive camera in it was hanging on a chair next to the sidewalk, a kid grabbed the bag and took off running, I saw right away, but it took me several seconds to accept the idea that someone was actually robbing me, so I stood up and ran after him, when I realized that I wasn't going to catch him, I cried out without believing it: "Stop thief, stop thief," he instantly dropped the bag. I do not remember whether I cried when I came back from a class ski trip and my parents announced to me that Pirouette, my hamster, had died while I was away. My father gave me a .22 rifle when I turned thirteen, which scared the rest of the family. I loved the smell of the cartridges for my rifle. I loved the shape of my rifle, but I was sorry it could only shoot one at a time, and I imagined that if our house was attacked I would have to think up a way to make the assailants think it was an automatic. Actually, my rifle only fired lead shot, not cartridges, which made it less injurious to human beings, including potential assassins. Although I don't hunt, my father gave me my grandfather's shotgun, I have sometimes considered using it to kill myself. I do more things when I haven't got much time than when I have lots. I dreamed that I was with my father, who was also Raphaël Ibañez, and we were walking through a lycée attended exclusively by tall blonde girls in Converse sneakers, then we bathed in a sweet stream and the streambed led to a cave that was carpeted with watercress that we ate all the way down to the bed before we went back to the lycée, full of desire. Riding in a car, I watch the power lines go up and down at the tops of the poles like strands of marshmallow in a French candy store. I find nature less hospitable than the city. I will take more interest in a house under construction than in a minimalist sculpture because, since the interest of the former is accidental, I feel more like the author than the viewer of the "work." One of my friends sang the first words of a chorus in

English, followed by a series of onomatopoeic sounds because that was where his comprehension ended. As a child I had a recurring nightmare: gravity has disappeared and humanity has drifted apart, my family have floated away and will never come back, everyone is the center of a universe that is infinitely expanding. Even if it is an odd sort of present, I thank my father and mother for having given me life. When I lie on the grass I remember the vertigo I felt at the age of six when, lying on the grass, I thought that if gravity stopped working, I would fall into the sky. I attended primary and secondary school in a reinforced concrete building that my friends and I called "Le Blockhaus," which explains why it took me years before I could look with pleasure at any building constructed of that material. I am friends with a couple who, in bed, play a game where they invent plausible names for Hollywood actors and actresses, I don't know what the prizes and penalties are. I draw better with my eyes closed than open. On the train I looked at the white hair of the passenger in front of me, he appeared above the headrest like an abstract ball of fur. When the sun goes down in the sea, I avoid looking at the band of reflections that connect me to it. I am rarely aboard a yacht.

I have not jet-skied. I can sail a dinghy or a catamaran. I went for a fifteen-day sail with friends in Brittany, I remember the days were long and never boring even though we did nothing except wait for the next port. I am not the right height for public seating, it's too small, which takes some of the pleasure out of movies and the theater and makes travel uncomfortable for me. I would like to communicate without using words or gestures, and just perceive everything that was in the brain of my interlocutor, like a photograph. Seeing Harlem from a train a sentence came into my head: "This is not the promised land." I have neither a hunting permit nor a gun permit. Even though the food is bland and more expensive than at other places, I eat in museum cafeterias, their minimalist décor, their luminosity, and the memory of the art I have just seen make up for their lack of character. I am thirty-nine at the moment I write these words. I have seen a work by Damien Hirst entitled *Armageddon*, made up of millions of flies stuck to a canvas several meters square. I drink more beer abroad than in France. My torso is longer than average. I have powerful legs. My fingers are thin but strong. I can snap my fingers, but also my toes. Since the age of fifteen I have been the same height but not the same weight. I have blue eyes, reddish-blond hair, my whiskers, body hair, and pubes are red. In summer my freckles spread, overlap, and give the illusion of a tan. I do not bite my nails, I cut them once a week. I do not wear pink shirts. I do not drink whiskey. I have sometimes drunk vodka, not with pleasure. I drink calvados. I drink a mixture of calvados and cassis, a recipe passed down from my grandfather whom I never knew. I have not taken the following courses, described in an American brochure for The Learning Annex: Succeed in Hollywood, Become the personal assistant to a celebrity while making good money and traveling the world with the rich and powerful, Speak about anything to anyone, Make money in special events and weddings, Open your own dry-cleaner's, Use hypnosis to raise sales, Become a superstar corporate "rainmaker," Draw with the right side of your brain, Make fifteen low-calorie and economical meals in just one evening, Learn to read music in one evening, Reverse the aging process through acupressure, Talk to your cat, Get a photographic memory in one evening, Get past procrastination now, Receive messages from the Beyond. I sometimes tell myself that if I lied things would be simpler, and not only for me. I hardly ever use matches, even for lighting the stove, I prefer electric lighters. I could not have worked in finance, accounting, I.T., scientific research, but I could have worked for an ecological party, in a humanitarian organization, a publishing house, or an arts institution. I look at geographical maps for pleasure, but I can do without a road map for planning a trip. On a geographical map, I begin by looking at the sea coasts, where the names are easiest to read, then I bury myself in the landmasses, without following any precise route, guided only by the capricious movement of my eyes. I wear sweaters with a zipper that I can zip up and down depending on the temperature. As a child I was convinced that I had a double on this earth, he and I were the same age, he had the same body, the same feelings I did, but not the same parents or the same background, for he lived on the other side of the planet, I knew that there was very little chance I would meet him, but still I believed that this miracle would occur. I fell out with a very close friend because for a few days he refused to come help me set up the computer that he'd sold me. I do not judge a country by the quality of its TV. A vacation in New York has tired me more than working in San Francisco. The first paintings I showed consisted of big canvases on which I'd dripped paint from top to bottom, and of simple geometrical forms made from a mixture of paint and sand the colors of earth or oxidized metals, this show took place in my uncle's gallery over three days in July 1993, I bought most of what was shown, I destroyed the others for lack of space. I painted from 1991 to 1996. I made five hundred paintings, I sold maybe sixty of them, roughly one hundred are stored in a maid's room in la Creuse, I burned the rest. Whether it's because I was tired of looking at them, or for lack of space, I felt a great relief when I burned my paintings. The pleasure principle guides my life more than the reality principle, although I am confronted more often by reality than by pleasure. As an artist and writer I could go crazy without noticing: I am indulged in all my eccentricities, since I work alone no one verifies what I do, it would take a while for people around me to notice that I'd gone around the bend, and, occasionally, to let me know. I sometimes wonder whether what I do is art or art therapy. When I was about fifteen, I bought two volumes from the "Que Sais-je?" series, one on art, the other on madness, these are still the subjects that trouble me the most. I have started *The Interpretation of Dreams* six times, I don't know why I've stopped. As a child, I liked to scare myself by fantasizing that someone (but who?) was making me scrape my fingernails down the length of my father's car. The prospect of a long walk in the mountains on a sunny day makes me euphoric. I forgive, and can even forget, wrongs done to me, but I have trouble forgiving a refusal to forgive. I understand punishment better than revenge. I am concerned with moral questions. I don't understand it when people avoid moral questions out of dandyism or what they consider broad-mindedness, and yet moralists strike me as either sad or reactionary. I have been to twenty-two countries: France, England, Switzerland, Germany, Spain, Italy, the United States, Portugal, Thailand, China, Russia, Finland, Holland, Greece, Luxembourg, Belgium, Poland, Czechoslovakia, Hungary, Hong Kong, Macao, India. The countries that made the biggest impression on me are India, where I traveled through the unreal, and the United States, where I traveled through movies. I have not set foot on the continents of Australia or Africa. At dinner I am not a performer, I can't be counted on to take the lead in conversation, but I make a good spectator, I laugh, I get surprised, I ask questions. At lunch I can be the performer if I am with one or two people, that is my maximum audience. At breakfast I'm alone even if I'm with someone else. In the morning it takes me two hours after I wake up for my brain to function normally. I go to bed around one in the morning, I fall asleep around two. I get up between eight and nine. I feel well, which means ready to work, between eleven-thirty and one-thirty, then from five o'clock in the afternoon until the moment I go to bed. I was born at three-ten in the afternoon, a time I hate, every day I am useless until five. The North makes me sad, the East frightens me, the West intimidates me, the South gladdens my heart. To play with the sun's reflection in a pocket mirror gives me a feeling of power. I love a Canadian accent, although I don't find it sexy in women. I always wonder whether the phone numbers on sex ads in the men's room are real, it would be easy to find out by trying them, I never have. I don't feel guilty for drinking too much wine, since it's an aristocratic thing to drink, but the opposite is true for beer, although it has fewer side effects. I complain, and complain about complaining. I laugh, and laugh because I'm laughing. I weep, and I do not weep from weeping, on the contrary, just knowing that I am weeping is enough to make me stop. I eat very little soup, and even less stew. Squash soup is the only soup that I ever want to prepare and eat. In Paris I never ride my bicycle anywhere just for pleasure, there has to be some practical reason. I am uneasy with new technologies, but in the end I adopt them. An astrologist friend told me that, according to my star chart, my weak spots were in my back and ears. I can't say I believe in astrology, but I can't say I don't. I would like to believe in ghosts. I would like to hum in the street as if I were alone. Nightclubs are sites of spectacle, I do not perform, I observe. Noisy restaurants make it impossible to have a conversation with my friends, and for me the point of dinner is to talk. I have sometimes had an idea for a book and discovered that it was a black and narrow room I could not escape, and conversely, I have sometimes discovered that it was a luminous house with an infinite number of wings where I could roam freely and at ease. It surprises me that my handwriting should have been fixed at a certain age, sixteen I think, and has never evolved since then. I invented a signature for myself at the age of thirteen, little knowing that I'd have the same one all my life. I wonder how Russians manage to be so Russian. In a café, I am more likely to sit at a table than stand at the bar. I do not go to a café in order to have conversations with others at the bar unless I am in a foreign country, I speak the language, and they have a bar in the back, only in Spain are all three conditions satisfied at once. A TV on in a café makes me turn around and leave. I wonder whether the landscape is shaped by the road, or the road by the landscape. I bought my first Levi's 501s at the age of fourteen at the Bon Fermier in Vernon, I was fascinated by the blue-gray cardboardy cotton and the button fly, putting them on I was leaping into time. I have not made love to a man. When I walk down the street, I do not look at my feet, I do not look at the surface they tread, I look at the facades as I pass them by, the upper stories rising above me, the road that lies before me. If I'm in a hurry, when I walk down the street, I don't see what I look at, the places, the people, and the objects are masses, abstract and colored, that I pass with indifference. Two politicians won my trust, Michel Rocard and François Bayrou, but they did not belong to the party I wanted to vote for. I vote for the Green party even though they rarely put forward a candidate I like. I have only a vague idea of the Green party's platform, I'm not sure they have clearer ideas than mine. I do not foresee making love with an animal. The eve of a long trip is filled with both exaltation and anxiety, but the day itself is a pure euphoria of action, and anxiety returns in the middle of the trip, at an empty moment, when the exoticism of the setting out has not yet given way to that of going home. On Dictaphone cassettes recorded a few moments before, I cannot listen to the content of the words, only the sound of my voice: I am less troubled by the doubling than by the disappearance of meaning. My voice recorded one minute ago on a Dictaphone sounds older than my voice recorded digitally five years before. My face filmed fifteen days ago on Super 8 looks older than my face filmed ten years before on a digital camera. I have on several occasions made love to two women at once. I have gone to swingers' clubs and I have joined in. When it comes to interior decoration, I do not like the colors orange, yellow, green, purple, and blue, only white, gray, brown, and red appeal to me. When I travel in a country where my cell phone doesn't work, it takes me two days to get used to its absence. When I travel in a country where my cell phone doesn't work, I have to wear a watch to know what time it is, it takes me two days to get used to it because I haven't worn a watch since I got a cell phone. When I come back from a long trip in a country where my cell phone didn't work, it takes me just a few minutes to get used to it again. I rarely know about the domestic policies of the countries where I travel. The only country whose domestic policies I know about is my own. I know nothing about the foreign policies of most countries, exceptions being the United States, Great Britain, and France. I know the name of five or six current presidents or prime ministers of other countries. If I drew the world from memory, I wonder how many countries I would leave out. I don't like the one they imposed on me, and yet I cannot imagine bearing a name besides my own. On a map I have an easier time picking out the American states than the African countries. I have made love to roughly fifty women, I wonder if that's a few or a lot. I have loved six women, four of them I told. I have cheated on a school exam. One night I went to a gay bar, where I stalked the back room, insatiably curious. I go to the pool in my neighborhood, I do not go to the pool when I am out of town. I have inherited lots of furniture that I didn't keep, I sold it, I have bought a sofa, I requisitioned some school chairs from the Cité Internationale one night with Yan Toma, I built one table, I bought another, I found a third one in the street, I replaced my bed with a mattress on the floor. I have kept, of the objects given to me by my family, only a few family portraits, some landscapes, a death's head, some taxidermy, some sculpture, a wooden pillar, a hunting rifle, some china, glasses, silverware, and a few bibelots, I don't keep them in my house, most are in a basement, I wouldn't miss them if I knew they stopped belonging to me. I can remember so well, years later, the face of someone I met only once that it can be awkward if the person remembers less of me than I do of him. I have sometimes asked the same question of someone several times, if the answer didn't interest me enough to remember it, it's only at the moment of hearing the answer that I remember having already asked. On the phone I find silence embarrassing. I want this epitaph engraved on my tombstone: "See you soon." The last time I learned something by heart was for a movie shoot and, before that, for a video, otherwise I have not learned anything by heart since I was in school. I write less easily at a round table, where my elbows hang in the void, than at a rectangular table, where they can bear my weight. For two years I painted round paintings that I did not show, soon afterward I stopped painting, since then looking at round paintings has made me sad. I do not take family photos, though I enjoy looking at the albums that my mother made when I was a child. I do not buy spiral notebooks because it is hard to write on the left-hand page, especially as your hand approaches the metal. When I was a child I once churned my yoghurt so hard with my spoon that it spattered all over the walls, my grandmother, usually so gentle, gave me a slap that left me stunned. When I was a child my mother sometimes called me Edouard the Stick (*le bâton*) because in the country I went around everywhere with a piece of wood, later, when I became a troublemaker, she called me the Tiresome Stick (*le bâton merdeux*), then, more simply, the Shit (*la merde*). I write more easily at night than in the daytime, until suddenly I realize it's over, exhaustion overwhelms me, I turn off the computer and go to bed. I connect easily with women, it takes longer with men. My best male friends have something feminine about them. I ride a motorcycle but I don't have the "biker spirit." I get bored as soon as a motorcyclist starts talking to me about technical things having to do with the engine, cylinders, speed, or mileage. I am an egoist despite myself, I cannot even conceive of being altruistic. My brother had two childhood friends, they were all about five years old, and he met them again when he was forty-five in Nice, where all three of them now live. I have no friends from my childhood. When I was a child, then a teenager, I had one best friend for two or three years, then another, and so on, I never kept a best friend more than four years, I was almost twenty before I had friends who lasted longer, and almost thirty before I met the friends I have now. I have been more faithful in friendship than in love, which isn't to say that I cheated on the women I was with, but that my relations with them lasted a shorter time than relations with my friends. In every friend I am looking for a brother. I have not found a friend in my brother, but I have not, alas, made the effort to look. My brother was too old for us to be friends. My brother and I are like night and day, and I may be the night. I have often thought that education had little influence over individuals, since my brother and I had the same education and have pursued divergent paths. I like my brother, this is probably reciprocal, I write "probably" because we have never discussed it. It moves me to see photos of my brother when he was little, I see that we have the same complexion, the same eyes, the same hair, but I know these similar envelopes contain minds that have never come into contact. At night it reassures me to hear a few quiet footfalls on the floor of the apartment above. I do not eat candy, it makes me sick. In a foreign city, I always feel an urge to visit the zoo, even though a foreign zoo is no more exotic than a French one. I start by looking up some precise information in a biographical dictionary, then I spend a much longer time flipping around. I prefer, in order, flipping around in an encyclopedia, a biographical dictionary, a normal dictionary, a French-English dictionary, a French-Spanish dictionary, a French-Latin dictionary. I sometimes flip around in a phone book for no special reason. I read synopses of movies in the paper without any intention of seeing them. I do not read the TV guide, I watch at random and find out what's on by channel-surfing. I watch movies on TV without planning to, so I rarely see one all the way through. I do not believe in the cinema of fiction, only four movies have made a deep impression on me, *Life Upside Down*, directed by Alain Jessua, *The Devil, Probably*, by Robert Bresson, and *The Mother and the Whore* and *Une sale histoire*, by Jean Eustache, certain other movies have distracted or moved me, but I don't give them the credit. I live with a feeling of permanent failure, although I don't fail especially often at things I try to do. I do not use an umbrella. I take little pleasure in success, failure leaves me cold, but it infuriates me never to have tried, when I could have. I go to the movies not to learn, but for distraction. I don't think movies are stupid, I just don't expect much from them. I believe more in literature, even minor literature, than in movies, even great ones. I don't have time to tell long stories. It takes me a while to realize that certain people bore me, such as people who are witty but tell stories slowly, with lots of useless details, at first I admire the precision of their memories, then I get tired, and finally I can't stand to wait fifteen minutes to find out the upshot of a story that should have taken one minute to tell. I went to Bordeaux for the first time when I was twenty-five, I found when I went back at the age of thirty-eight that I remembered nothing: not a street, not a museum, not a café, not a river, nothing. There are periods when I remember everything, and others when my memory fails me, I don't remember things I know perfectly well, I can't think of the name of the place Vendôme or the title of a novel by Stendhal. I think the big toe is doomed to disappear. I feel uneasy in a tall chair, I need low seats in order to sit up straight without making an effort. I feel better sitting in a hard chair than in a soft chair. I do not keep my clothes in a wardrobe but on open shelves so I can take them in at one glance. Twice in my life I have been courted by gay men, they knew I wasn't gay, I did not give them satisfaction. I have never been attracted to a man, which is a shame, the gay life appeals to me. As far as I know, I have no children. I got one woman pregnant, we decided that she would have an abortion, this was painful for her, as it was for me, she told me it was worse for her, meaning I would never understand. The first time I made love to a woman it was her first time too, but she seemed to be a natural. In contemporary art, I would tend to gravitate toward people who are nice, the trouble is that nice people are nice to everyone, they like everyone, which diminishes the value of their judgments. On the boulevard Saint-Michel I saw an unusually tall man, his head, which rose above the crowd, was not like a human face, he had a few tufts of hair, two holes instead of a nose, no ears or lips, some bits of tooth emerged from a gaping rictus, his face was askew, all the skin was burned, only his eyes had a normal shape, but the expression in them was frightened, as if the passing crowd were looking and making fun of him, this was twenty-five years ago, I remember it as if I had seen him just now. Certain knapsacks are too short and hurt my back, others, better designed, do it good. In the sheets of cheap hotels I have sometimes found body hairs belonging to previous guests. In cheap hotels, the zones of doubtful cleanliness I most distrust are the carpet, the sheets and the pillow cases, the toilet seat, and the TV remote. I sometimes sleep in hotels I don't like, but there are no other hotels for miles around, I don't know their addresses and it's the middle of the night. One day, in an American motel, I saw the following price list: double room sixty dollars, single room fifty-five dollars, three hours thirty-eight dollars. I cannot remember attending a Mass that didn't bore me. Until the age of twelve I thought I was gifted with the power to shape the future, but this power was a crushing burden, it manifested itself in the form of threats, I had to take just so many steps before I reached the end of the sidewalk or else my parents would die in a car accident, I had to close the door thinking of some favorable outcome, for example passing a test, or else I'd fail, I had to turn off the light not thinking about my mother getting raped, or that would happen too, one day I couldn't stand having to close the door a hundred times before I could think of something good, or to spend fifteen minutes turning off the light the right way, I decided enough was enough, let everything fall apart, I didn't want to spend my life saving other people, that night I went to bed sure the next day would bring the Apocalypse, nothing happened, I was relieved but a little bit disappointed to discover I had no power. When I do karate, it makes me euphoric to fight invisible enemies. I went out with a woman who sometimes would threaten to leave me as a way of making me say I loved her, all I had to do was get annoyed and say "I love you" and instantly she was all smiles. I would like to go to Japan before I die, but something tells me I won't. I would be very moved if a friend told me he loved me, even if he told me more out of love than friendship. As a child I dreamed of being, not a fireman, but a veterinarian, the idea was not my own, I was imitating my cousin. I played house with a girl cousin, but there were variants, it could be doctor (formal inspection of genitals), or thug and bourgeoise (mini rape scene). When we played thug and bourgeoise, my cousin would walk past the swing set where I'd be sitting, outside our family's house, I would call out to her in a menacing tone of voice, she wouldn't answer but would act afraid, she would start to run away, I would catch her and drag her into the little pool house, I would bolt the door, I'd pull the curtains, she would try vaguely to get away, I would undress her and simulate the sexual act while she cried out in either horror or pleasure, I could never tell which it was supposed to be, I forget how it used to end. I am making an effort to specialize in me. If I am not the victim, the suspicions of other people make me laugh. To ease my backache after I've been driving a long way, I lie down on a hard floor, arms crossed, legs slightly raised. In Thailand, in a compartment on a train to Chiang Mai, I fell asleep sitting up, I woke to the sound of my own snoring, seeing the smiles of the friends who were with me, I was ashamed of the noises I could have made, but I will never know what they were. I have spent several idle days on a beach in Thailand, in the sun, on a white sandy beach, the water was turquoise, I slept in a straw hut, I ate fish in the sun, I did nothing, I only soaked up that ecstasy like a blessing. In la Creuse, in Bost-Boussac, at the large isolated house where my grand-mother lived, it was three o'clock on a hot, sunny August afternoon and a friend and I were looking out over the countryside, drowsy from a long lunch and the Bordeaux we'd had with it, a couple was coming down the road that led to the house, a black man in his fifties wearing a Haitian shirt, gray trousers, and a cowboy hat, followed by a timid woman, maybe sixty years old, who wore a black dress and big glasses, the man smiled all the way from the end of the road to the house, the woman struggled and panted to keep up, he took off his hat, he shook my hand saying: "Hello, I'm Monsieur Macabre, but I am very much alive," and he burst out laughing, then went on: "Messieurs, what do you think of God?": he was a Jehovah's Witness. I used to think I knew very little about things to do with me. At a window with small window-panes, my eye sees the wooden frame more than the landscape. At a picture window, my eye sees nothing but landscape. In Corsica, a friend and I played an Oulipian game, N+7, which consists of replacing each noun in a text with the noun that comes seven places later in the dictionary, I chose an instruction manual for a washing machine, we started in the middle of the afternoon and near midnight, by the light of the moon, we were still helpless with laughter whenever we repeated the sentence: "Set head cold to star key to ensure mixing of chiropractor and Tahitian." I have flat feet. My coccyx sticks out farther than I would like, if I sit too long in a certain position it hurts like a useless tail. Having flat feet annoys me for two reasons: I can't wear shoes with arched soles, and if I walk barefoot and it's burning hot, my whole foot suffers, not just the extremities that support it. One day I told my analyst: "I don't take any pleasure in what I have," and I wept. On the radio I heard a program where a very witty woman told some out-of-date anecdotes, and it was not until the interviewer named his interlocutor that I realized they were talking about Jean d'Ormesson. I saw a TV program where Frédéric Beigbeder invited some naked writers onto the set, but they were posed in such a way that you couldn't see their dicks. I saw Charles Bukowski only once on TV, in that famous clip from *Apostrophes* where he walked off the set, drunk. I discovered the face of Ray Bradbury on a TV screen in a motel near Stockholm, New Jersey: he was wearing a blue shirt with a white collar, a brown tie and beige suspenders, but his legs were bare, he was wearing shorts and sneakers, his old white hair was combed over to hide his bald scalp, one of his eyes was stuck shut, and the other looked far away behind the corrective lens of his thick glasses, at first I was frightened by the old man's appearance and his cavernous voice, I wondered whether I would go on TV if

I were in his place, then I admired this American way of dealing with his decrepitude. When I am away and I'm writing in the evening in a hotel room, and it's time to go out to dinner, I know that when I come back I won't go back to work, but I always convince myself otherwise so I can eat without feeling guilty. I wonder why wallpaper tends, in general, to be ugly. I feel uneasy about wall-to-wall carpets, which gather dust and stains, especially in hotels where I imagine they contain all the miasmas of previous guests, without quite knowing what I mean by "miasmas." I bought a pornographic magazine in a convenience store, at the register I was less embarrassed than I had thought I would be, the cashier, an Indian, picked it up and folded it in such a way that the other customers in line wouldn't see what it was, he slid it into a brown paper bag, I could read nothing in his face, neither complicity nor reproach. When I drive a car for more than an hour several days in a row, my lower back aches, which doesn't happen with a motorcycle. On a motorcycle I go faster than in a car, especially on the highway, to kill the boredom. On a motorcycle, on the highway, once the vibrations and fatigue and the unrolling asphalt have grown hypnotic, time no longer counts, and boredom, which exists only as a function of measurement, disappears. I find certain ethnicities more beautiful than others. I don't write in the morning, my brain isn't up to it yet, I don't write in the afternoon, I'm too sad, I write from five o'clock on, I need to have been awake a long time, my body relaxed from a day's fatigue. If it's sunny out and I spend all day roaming the streets looking for subjects to photograph, then when night falls I come home harassed by a sweet fatigue, eyes aching from too much light, I go to bed exhausted, in the blackness the day's images file past like a random diorama until sleep knocks me out, the next day I wake up with circles under my eyes, as if I've been punished by the organs I abused. When I read the descriptions in a guidebook, I compare them to the reality, I'm often disappointed since they are fulsome, otherwise they wouldn't be there. Days when I play sports I feel guilt-free, even in domains that have nothing to do with the body. Although I have written mainly on the computer for the last few years, my right middle finger still has a callous where I hold my pen. Although I have published two books with him, my publisher continues to introduce me as an artist, if I were an accountant as well as a writer, I wonder whether he would introduce me as an accountant. In the jokes I heard at school that involved competitions between different nationalities, the Frenchman always had the slowest car, the gun that jammed, or the smelliest underpants. In Spain twenty years ago, I was invited by a friend of a friend, my traveling companion, to spend an evening at the home of a seventy-year-old man, German by birth, our conversation was relaxed and funny, I felt happy, it was summer, I was on vacation, we were drinking good wine, platters of spicy food were served on a terrace overlooking the sea, the conversation took an unexpected turn as the man began to express more and more reactionary views in a charming tone of voice, he smiled as he looked into my eyes for approbation, the socialist-communist menace, the longhairs, the Jews, the unemployed, the homosexuals, he covered them all, he was trying to take me hostage with his hospitality, I was more perverse than he was, I smiled so that he would reveal himself, which he did beyond reason, when we left the table he took me to see his son's bedroom, there was a Nazi flag thumbtacked to the wall, he admiringly singled out several books on the shelves, including *Mein Kampf*, I was astonished, looking back, that the friend of a friend, who knew what sort of man this was, a retired SS officer, had accepted his invitation. I do not tell jokes. There is no single word, there are only circumlocutions, to describe a situation in which I found myself: the woman I was seeing got pregnant by me, then she had an abortion, whereas I wasn't pregnant, I was seeing a woman who was pregnant by me, then I didn't have an abortion, but I was "someone seeing a woman who has aborted the child of his that she was carrying": a word for her, a heavy formula for me. I accumulate beginnings. When I was thirteen, on a ski trip to Val-d'Isère, I went back to the chalet to get my sunglasses in the middle of the morning, I took off my snow boots, I went into the dormitory in my socks, not making any noise, there I surprised a forty-something counselor in the middle of masturbating a ten-year old boy who had to stay in bed because he'd broken his leg, the counselor snatched back his hand and smoothed down the sheet, and that night, while he made his rounds between the beds for lights-out, I called out across the dormitory: "I'm sure he hasn't got any underpants on under his sweat suit," right as he was passing me, I pulled down his pants, he was naked, he blushed and ran out without saying anything to me, for the rest of the trip he went to great lengths to make sure our paths never crossed and our eyes never met. I couldn't say whether I'd prefer to have my left arm amputated or my right leg. When I read psychiatric manuals, I often find that I have one symptom of the illnesses they describe, sometimes more than one, sometimes every symptom. I do not write in order to give pleasure to those who read me, but I would not be displeased if that is what they felt. I can tear a piece of writing paper folded in two, in four, in eight, in sixteen, in thirty-two, in sixty-four, but no more. For reading, my favorite positions are, in order: lying down, sitting in an armchair, sitting on a sofa, sitting at a table, standing up. Often I think I know nothing about myself. I cannot bring myself to hate Jacques Chirac. I like to watch a plastic bag flying around between office buildings, especially when you can't tell whether it's going up or going down. When I ask for directions, I am afraid I won't be able to remember what people tell me, I especially dread those useless directions that consist of people saying, "Then you'll see a pizzeria, that's not the place." I am always shocked when people give me directions and they actually get me where I'm going: words become road. I like slow motion because it brings cinema close to photography. I get along well with old people. I have yet to meet an old man who still listens to rock, but then I haven't met any old men who listened to rock when they were young. To feel pity makes me sad, but to be the object of someone else's pity makes me sadder. I have missed two important meetings for the same reason, one with the Polish minister of culture, whom I was supposed to interview, the other with an American judge, whom I was supposed to photograph, I showed up late because I lost track of time. When I was eighteen, I showed up late to a history class, the teacher didn't scold me directly, but he shared this verdict with the class: "Those who arrive late in youth arrive late all their lives." On a trip, I fold my dirty laundry so it will take up less space. I could not be the same person in another body. I cannot bear to think about the death of someone I love, when the person dies I suffer two losses: the person is dead, and the unthinkable has occurred. I remember my dreams better when they are useful for my work. I love to recall my dreams, no matter what is in them. My dreams are structured so much like memories of things that happened in real life, sometimes I wonder whether they didn't. If I sleep badly, I dream more, or else I remember my dreams better. I do not interpret dreams. My dreams are as strange to me as those of other people. It makes me laugh when people tell their dreams. On several different tables at my high school I read these sentences, written one above the other: "God is dead (Nietzsche). Nietzsche is dead (God)." I do not sleep under a comforter but under blankets, which I pull up if I get cold, a comforter rarely produces the right temperature. I have insulted just one person, the cultural councilor at the consulate where I did my military service. My memory embellishes. I often apologize, always thinking I shouldn't, and that I shouldn't have to. Over one summer I got six tick bites, only four years later did I become convinced that I had contracted Lyme disease, after I read a list of the symptoms on a Web site. I have cheated on schoolwork, but not at games. I dine alone in a restaurant if I have no choice, which happens only on trips. To dine alone in a restaurant seems paradoxical to me: going out to a restaurant is festive, festivities are collective. To find out whether I was homosexual, I tried to masturbate while thinking of men, it didn't work. When I watch the hunting show *Très Chasse*, I have the impression that the hunters feel no guilt after the orgasm of the shot. I thank people easily. Ever since I saw *Jaws*, I have been unable to swim in the sea without thinking about the sharks that may be on their way to get me. One hot dry summer, my mother read to me from the book *Alive* every night after dinner, it was an account of a plane crash in the Cordillera, in the Andes, the survivors ate the bodies of the others in order to stay alive, I was eleven, I don't know why my mother read me this story. I have seen several of the *Friday the Thirteenth* movies, after the one called *Friday the Thirteenth: The Final Chapter*, in which Jason dies, I thought that was the end of it, but a new episode came out, *Friday the Thirteenth: A New Beginning*. I try to write prose that will be changed neither by translation nor by the passage of time. I like to finish a task on time, that is, when the big hand of the clock is on the twelve. I do not think I have inspired pity. In Vieux-Boucau I tried to surf one afternoon, without success, I had no intuitive sense of how it ought to be done, or of the pleasure I'd feel if I did it right. One July I passed someone who had a face like the Elephant Man's, I was on my bike, I was going fast, I thought I had hallucinated it, I turned around to catch up with him, I hadn't been wrong, but when I see something exceptional, I think for the first few moments that it's an illusion. A woman's breasts may hold my attention to the point that I can't hear what she's saying. I wish I were the singer in a rock band. I do not wish I were an anchorman. Out of curiosity I accept the first invitation to dinner with people who I already know are going to bore me, but the subsequent ones I decline. When something wonderful takes me by surprise, I try to reproduce the circumstances under which it occurred, in order to make it happen again, but that is confusing the thing with the grace of accident. A friend of a friend claimed that she could return to an interrupted dream, once she had woken up, by going back to sleep, she also claimed that she could intervene consciously, while she was sleeping, in the contents of her dreams and return to her favorite moments. I do not always choose the best moment for saying good-bye in a public place to someone who is busy with something else, sometimes the person doesn't hear me, so I try again, hoping no one else has overheard. I was speaking with a friend, who was very beautiful but distant, when some snot lodged itself on the edge of her nostril, ever since this anodyne event I have found her less distant, although her behavior hasn't changed. I have sometimes looked under the bed before I got into it. I regret not having been born in 1945, I would have been twenty-three in 1968, I would have lived through the sexual revolution and believed in various utopias during the 1970s, I would have made a lot of money in the 1980s, which I would have happily spent in the 1990s, and then I would have enjoyed a comfortable retirement full of happy memories in the 2000s, unfortunately I was born in 1965 and I was twenty during the 1980s, indisputably the ugliest years since the end of the Second World War. When I walk down the street, the words on signs and in shop windows get mixed up in my head and turn into absurd slogans. I would forgive a woman for cheating on me if the other man was better than I am. I like the smell of my hair, even dirty. It amazes me that I can lift my arm without understanding how my brain transmits the order. I am always telling myself that I ought to write positive things, and I do, but it's harder than writing negative things. In a sandwich, I don't see what I am eating, I imagine it. When I am in front of the TV I don't enjoy what I eat because I don't look at it. Even when I'm very tired, I can watch TV for several hours. I had an idea for a bad video: to humiliate a turkey by having it walk around in public in a T-shirt bearing the face of Jacques Chirac. When I'm in a foreign country, I do things that I would never dare to do in my own country, because everything seems like fiction. Since I started writing on a computer, I have saved everything I write by hand. I do not dream of flying. In the middle of summer, a rainy day makes me as happy as a sunny day in the middle of winter. When I'm in a foreign country, I pay more attention to the norm than to the exceptions, I would rather spend time in small cities that have nothing remarkable about them than in capitals full of curiosities. I have not put on rubber boots in at least three years. I suppress the superfluous. I am handsomer with a cane. I don't need to talk much. I need to not talk much. I do not shout. I eat three times a day. I do not eat between meals. I drink two liters of tea a day. I need to leave the house at least once a day. Once when I was six I was running up the boulevard Saint-Michel, I was racing my cousin back to school, each of us on his own sidewalk, I crossed without looking, a car hit me, I flew two meters and landed on my head, nose broken, face bloody, the car drove off, someone got the license number, the driver was a nursing student, my father went to see her, he had decided not to lodge a complaint because he didn't want to ruin her future career, she wouldn't see him, she lived with her mother who opened the door a crack and said: "If you've come to blackmail us, get lost," and slammed it shut. When I was fourteen I had my ears pinned back, at the suggestion of my father, who had his ears pinned back when he was eighteen. When I was twelve I had warts on my left heel, several treatments failed to get rid of them, my mother decided to have them burned off, a very painful operation that my brother was supposed to have undergone a few years earlier, but the day before the operation, his terror had literally made the warts disappear, I hoped the same thing would happen to me, but it didn't, the dermatologist worked away at my foot for an hour, when we left his office my mother said, "I think I suffered worse than you did," two months later the warts came back, one year later another dermatologist, whom I trusted the moment I saw him because of his gentle face, made them disappear in four sessions by applying a brown odorless cream that he had concocted himself, I learned ten years later that he died of AIDS. I have Asian friends. I do not eat ice cream. I do not fill my house with "finds." In nearly empty restaurants I count the number of people and pity the fate of the restaurateurs. I cannot stand to read vernacular English translated into French, the expressions, often misplaced, are dredged up from the translator's youth or from what he believes to be the language of the street. I enjoy the simple décor of Protestant temples. I admire American religious ceremonies where the preachers launch into sermons that come close to song and trance, as if they might revive that morbid, desireless event: the Mass. In my periods of depression, I visualize the funeral after I kill myself, there are lots of friends there, lots of sadness and beauty, the event is so moving that it makes me want to live through it, so it makes me want to live. I don't know how to leave naturally. I want to laugh with common people, tattooed, fat, bare-chested in a campground, making lots of noise and off-color remarks. I shave with an electric razor, it's quicker and less painful than a blade. I often wonder what people say about me right after I leave: maybe nothing. I have had four motorcycles: a Kawasaki Zephyr 750, a Yamaha SR 125, a Honda CB 500, a Kawasaki ER 500. I do not write memoirs. I do not write novels. I do not write short stories. I do not write plays. I do not write poems. I do not write mysteries. I do not write science fiction. I write fragments. I do not tell stories from things I've read or movies I've seen, I describe impressions, I make judgments. It is no use asking me to repeat a news story, even one a few weeks old. I don't learn the names of cabinet ministers by heart. I learned what little I know about agropolitics in prep school. I visit numerous buildings though I have no technical knowledge of architecture, it amazes me that they can construct a vault, a ceiling twenty meters high, a tunnel, a skyscraper, I don't want to know any more about it because I'm afraid I will be disenchanted. I know nothing about the mechanics of automobiles, but I am not amazed that cars go. I would like to accept the idea of love without passion. Sports on TV bore me. Concerts on TV bore me. I find the musicians badly dressed, with bad haircuts. I do not go to concerts. I have a recurring nightmare: in an apartment where I've been living for several years I find a hole in a room that I rarely use, the hole is accessible from outside, so all that time anyone could have come in without my knowing it, and maybe they have. I prefer lamps with lampshades to halogen lamps. Someone playing the saw depresses me more than the accordion, but less than clowns. The traditional circus revolts me more than figure skating. I can manage to snicker at synchronized swimming, but not at figure skating. In curling, the sweeper makes me laugh. I feel sorry for actors who have reinvented themselves as Renaissance jesters in sound and light shows, especially if they take their job seriously. I have witnessed an air guitar competition. I find mimics reactionary. I would rather watch bad mimics, who think they are doing impressions of celebrities but only mimic other mimics. In disused factories and abandoned barns I feel emotions that are aesthetic (beauty defined by function), nostalgic (sites of production where nothing now is produced), erotic (memories of children's games), beneficent vacuity, calm, all mixed up, in a tingling way, with feelings of death, fear (perfect scene for a crime), and the forbidden (no one gave me permission to enter this private property). I always regret taking a shower at night, the hot water keys me up and keeps me from sleeping. I feel irritable and sticky if I don't wash in the morning. My oldest memory is of a creek in Spain with a high, steep bank, I am wearing a white hat and I don't know how to swim, according to my mother this happened when I was less than two years old. The ticking of the alarm clock and the dripping of radiators keep me from sleeping. I sleep better in absolute darkness. I have dry skin. As a hypochondriac, I rejoice in my ignorance of most diseases. I drink water. I do not drink lemonade. I drink Coca-Cola.

I do not drink beer. I drink red wine when I eat, and sweet whites by themselves. I often remember that there is something I'm forgetting, but what? I prefer beginnings to endings. I do not scorn the teachings of my mother. I have not managed to describe the pain of a powerful electric shock. I am surprised that some people worship Satan, the name makes you think more of profanation than of cults. I have taken Prozac, Lysanxia, Athymil, Lexomil, and Temesta without success. I have stolen things from shops, but not from people's homes. I have never swindled anyone. I do not feel joy doing evil. I saw a madman walking up the boulevard Beaumarchais in his socks, in the middle of the street, creating a traffic jam that moved as slowly as he did, he wore white and gazed up at the sky, trailed by the furious honking cortege of cars, it wasn't until he got to place de la République that he deigned to step up onto the sidewalk. When I lived in the rue Legendre I often saw a woman in her sixties who was a mass of nervous tics, I wondered how she managed to smoke without burning herself. Three things make pools unpleasant: the locker rooms, the fluorescent lights, the smell of chlorine. I have no financial woes. I wait to sort my mail. My life is nothing like a hammer. I wish there were one-liter bottles of wine. In an abandoned factory, I smelled a mixture of dust, grease, old floor-boards, and fossilized sweat. I think the rich are wickeder than the poor. "I love you" can be a form of blackmail. I do not force myself to be enthusiastic, even with people who are. I have spoken with several American Indians. I have spoken with several Indian Indians. I have spoken with at least a thousand Americans. I have no obese friends. I have no anorexic friends. I cannot integrate my-self into a group of friends who already know each other, I will always be the latecomer, I like groups of friends formed all together at the same moment. I do not know what I expect from love. Passionate declarations make me think of hysteria. A friend of mine swears that people be-have more aggressively toward him when he wears his red suit. Here is how I tell the story of Jesus: an adulteress got her husband to believe that she was impregnated by God, she drove her son crazy with this story, which he believed, he set off to announce the good news and it got him killed. I have sometimes thought that everything I know is stored in my brain, so I think intensely about this flimsy piece of flesh, but I feel a void, the organ evokes nothing in me: I am unable to think about the organ of my thinking. I do not iron my shirts. I do not think my house is tilting to its death. Too much light doesn't bother me during the day, but it gives me neuralgia at night. I have no spiritual father. I do not know what debts I owe to which artists. I do not feel myself under the influence of any writer. I am more guest than host. I do not wear tight pants, they prevent me from writing. I will never have finished reading the Bible. I will never be done with *In Search of Lost Time*, when I get to the end, I've forgotten the beginning, starting again doesn't change that. I admire Douglas Huebler and Edward Ruscha. I admire Walker Evans, Diane Arbus, Stephen Shore, and Joel Sternfeld. If I have an idea in mind for a piece and it turns out already to exist, I don't abandon it, the piece is not the idea. I can't read a stolen book. I like the flat style of police reports. I feel Manichean. A friend of mine attributes his suicide attempts to his having been a battered child. I have utterly lost touch with friends who were dear to me, without knowing why, I believe they don't know why themselves. In a Chinese pharmacy I thought I read on one of the bottles "octopus wigs." At the cocktail hour I drink tea. I drink Lapsang Souchong, Yunnan, Keemun, Hojicha. In the morning I drink a glass of orange juice, I eat yoghurt, I drink half a liter of tea. I prefer the name to the taste of Darjeeling. I notice the length of a journey less if I already know the way. I have lived through 14,370 days. I have lived through 384,875 hours. I have lived through 20,640,000 minutes. I am one meter and eighty-six centimeters tall. My eye is not sated with seeing, nor my ear with hearing. Déjà vu gives me more pleasure than a great wine. Suburban on- and off-ramps stress me out, though I rarely lose my way. I am proud to go to a rock concert, and a little bit ashamed of going to a concert of classical music. The polished audiences at jazz concerts bore me. The old white California jazz musicians are antithetical to the idea I have of jazz. I have a fantasy involving female art students. I was not an art student. Everything I know about art I learned on my own. I do not get tired of taking pictures. I do not listen to opera. I prefer chamber music to symphonies. My favorite instrument is the cello, I deplore the dearth of solo pieces for cello. I play the piano. I may get up on a trampoline some day. I have made one parachute jump, it took longer to talk about than to do. The smoke of a blond cigarette coughed out by a woman sitting near me on a lawn in summer has left me enchanted. I photograph more old men than children, which violates the norms of family albums. I have had several cars without ever worrying about their technical performance. I have bought only used cars. Love does not distinguish me. I do not like the smell of vinyl car seats when it rains. Only once did I buy a new vehicle: a motorcycle, Kawasaki ER 500. I have not written fewer postcards since the appearance of the Web. I am writing this book on a computer, there will never be a manuscript. I seem too nice for mean girls to like me. I have sometimes taken pictures knowing in advance that they would be bad. I listen to music better through headphones than at a concert. I see a movie better at the movie theater than on TV. I am more attentive to the script of a play when I read it than when I see it performed. I've been to the opera only once, it was one time too many, after that I refused the invitation of generous friends to come see a production of *Madama Butterfly* at the Verona amphitheater, answering only: "I do not like opera." I can't read big books lying down: it tires my arms and crushes my stomach. At night I eat too much. I feel that I've eaten too much more often than not enough. I never regret not having had dinner. In a car I prefer entering a tunnel to leaving one, on a motorcycle the opposite. I spent a long time trying to like plastic furniture. I do not like being the center of attention. I do not monopolize the conversation. I sigh inwardly when someone begins to tell a joke. It never occurs to me to go to the movies and see a comedy. I do not see action movies. I do not see Westerns. I like the idea of science fiction, but not its literary or cinematic productions. I would be curious to see a pornographic science fiction movie. I would be curious to see a Shakespeare play performed by figure skaters. I would be curious to see a tragic movie performed by comic actors. I would be curious to see a dance piece performed by people who don't have dancers' bodies. I would be curious to see a show of paintings curated by celebrities who think they know about painting. I was passing a gallery that I did not know had gone out of business, from the sidewalk I saw an installation that instantly made me want to go inside, a mannequin crudely costumed as an apostle was spreading the gospel to other mannequins gathered around him in supposedly period clothes, there were, for some reason, a plough, a cuckoo clock, and a poster of Jamaica, it wasn't until I went inside that I realized the gallery had been replaced by a Mormon temple, and that the "installation" was not a parody. Fortunately,

I do not know what I expect from life. I am afraid of the gaze of hypnotists, even in photos. I sometimes meet people who I think have hypnotic powers, then I have to perform a ritual to escape from their sorcery: blink and draw my head back. French words pronounced by Americans make me laugh. Poor people do not frighten me. My parents do not stifle me. Potatoes put me to sleep. An American friend has an LP entitled *Music to Help You Stop Smoking*, among the pieces is a Chopin-Tchaikovsky medley. I had the idea of doing a *Self-Portrait with Candy*, in which my upper lip would bulge from the hard candy tucked inside it. If, lying on my back, I look at a woman's face upside down, her chin becomes a monstrous nose, and her mouth looks like a deformed person's, when she speaks, the inverse motion of her lips distracts me from what she is saying. I don't get the same odor from an English lawn as from a French one. In a landscape, things in the distance tell me no stories. When I was young I was obsessed with a series of photographs by a photographer whose name I never knew, you saw Jesus come back in the form of a hippie and get beaten to death, years later I discovered the photographs of Duane Michals, which I loved, but it was a long time before I found out that he was also the author of the series entitled *Christ in New York*. In foreign countries the street is an exhibition. The lists of things I have to do are too long. When I lie down in a public place, park or beach, I stretch out, arms crossed, legs slightly apart, I look like a corpse or a Christ fallen out of the sky, eventually someone comes over and asks whether I'm all right. Everything I write is true, but so what? At the supermarket in a foreign country I always think of the Clash song "Lost in the Supermarket." It's harder for me to eat bad food than to look at a bad painting. I used to play pool. I used to play knucklebones, I remember the big bridge, the little bridge, the death's head, and many other throws whose names I have forgotten. Playing Monopoly, I used to lose to my brother, I thought it was because he was older, I found out years later that he was cheating as the banker. I used to play Parcheesi, Gooses Wild, Mille Bornes, checkers, chess, gin, liars' poker, strip poker, war, Monopoly, Clue. Board games start off by boring me and end up getting on my nerves. I cannot remember a single game of Monopoly that didn't end with all the players sick of it. I took a trip that lasted three months, during which I slept a lot and worked, which got me out of a depression that lasted a year, during which I slept badly and worked very little. In the space of one Sunday in Syracuse I met an unusual number of strangers who talked too much to me. In a crowd I am more alone than I am by myself. In a small town I can't go for a long aimless walk. I do not go walking in crowds to find models for my photographs, for despite the increased abundance of choice, the faces pass too quickly for me to desire them. I find the old, the fat, the poor, and the deformed more photogenic than the young, the thin, the rich, and the good-looking, but I am wary of their distinguishing features: I prefer to take pictures of average people, on whom the marks of life are more subtle, so in this sense, I am more interested in photographing the secretary in an insurance office than someone obese with one eye and tattoos. In the United States, with a few simple formalities I could change my name in an hour or two, and soon I'd have accomplished a project impossible in France: to become Anne Onymous. I wouldn't want to die of drunkenness in a wine vat. In one of my recurring nightmares, gravity is so heavy that the chubby pseudo-humans who wander the empty surface of the earth move in slow motion through an endless moonlit night. When I think it's going to rain I take along a hat to shield my glasses. I end a trip abroad when I stop seeing ordinary objects as curiosities. I think Sunday is an old day. I do not count calories. I do not pay attention to the nutritional properties of what I eat, all I pay attention to is my taste and my appetite. I am not on a diet. I am wary of any driver who keeps his hat on behind the wheel. When I was a child, I was afraid of being kidnapped. Purées frustrate me because they have no crunch. I do not know what prudence means. Intense sensations tire me out more quickly than subtle ones. The lives of celebrities interest me less than the lives of the unknown. I do not believe anyone has ever cast a spell on me. When I drive on the highway, I spend too much time looking at the cracks. I recollect more than I collect. I have not suffered from a skin rash. I am wary of benches. I do not "splash water on my face," I wash. I don't say "automobile," I say "car." I do not need to make third parties acknowledge a romantic connection. I do not imagine my own wedding. I prefer dogs to cats. I do not have a maid. I do not say, "How exquisite." I don't like it when people just drop in. In the morning I do sixty pushups and one hundred leg lifts. I eat the flesh of a grape, I spit out some of the seeds. Peach fuzz makes my teeth grate. I do not count the number of cherries I eat. Parties are sometimes an ordeal. The word "machination" triggers my paranoia. I do not hate. I am entranced by the indiscretions of strangers. I admire the ingenuity of traps. Drugstores didn't lose their sinister allure when I learned that they are not where you buy drugs. Low necklines excite me. My all-time favorite title is *Death Threat with Orchestra*, by Xavier Boussiron. I feel handsomer after I go to the beach than before. After a shampoo, I make cranial music by running my fingers through my wet hair. Lying on the ground, I see the house upside down. The quest for prestige makes me feel pity. I appreciate silent parlor magicians. I stick with my first impression. My unconscious is quicker and more often correct than my conscious. I do not use adjectives as nouns. I have never broken my leg. To me, "too late an hour" means in the morning. Hearing a compulsive liar gives me a secret pleasure. I am not depressed when I travel. If I spend a long time bent over, and stand up, I see stars. I do not use the word "cardigan." I do not have breakfast in bed. Peanut butter and shrimp puffs give me dry mouth. I avoid abbreviations. I lean over a balcony railing to watch people from above, but I don't know where I could lean to see them from below. I have never petted a panther. I used to have a Mexican costume. I pay homage to Suzanne Salmet. I cook with basil, tarragon, coriander. I am thin. I don't sweat much. The more I know about an author, the less I mythologize him. The palm of my hand ages less quickly than my face. I penetrate a woman faster than I pull out. If I kiss for a long time, it hurts the muscle under my tongue. I have never been sodomized. A woman slapped me. I have never been punched. I sleep on my side. I sometimes wake up in the same position as when I went to sleep. I wonder where I will die. On the edge of a precipice, I get a rush from the space and I tremble at the void. When I have vertigo, I fall in my mind. My registered letters contain bad news. I do not see omens. I do not mutilate myself. I do not like show tunes. It wouldn't occur to me to tap-dance. I would be perfectly happy to live the same life a second time, but not a third. The first day of snow is a holiday. Lakes attract me, the sea repels me, ponds leave me cold. I do not wear more than two colors at a time. Cumin reminds me of armpits. If not for the smell, I wouldn't mind throwing up. I'm talkative for the first fifteen minutes. I do not know the name of the color I see behind my eyelids. I would believe more in God if it were a Goddess. I have nothing to say about cisterns. I find winks unsettling. I love the sound of the wind and the noise of the rain. My voice carries less in the snow. I know how much I'm seen, but not how much I'm understood. Apart from maybe ten countries, I don't know anything about national literatures, I know nothing, for example, about the literature of Honduras, Angola, Pakistan, or the Philippines. I look at the sky in a puddle. I fantasize about skateboards, trampolines, surfing, and paragliding. Soccer, running, tennis and golf bore me. When I was a child I did not choose what I ate. Pink flamingos look unreal to me. Some friends consider me obsessive. I do not trust untranslatable texts. Bad weather makes me glad. I do not try to be first. If I write in ink and my note-book falls in the water, everything blurs. I still laugh over the phrasing of that advertisement "Mammouth is flat-tening its prices." I am in favor of banning four-by-fours in cities. Sore throats and colds help me write. For me *Ginette, musette, fillette, trompette* all evoke a single universe. I have not been spanked. I am easily hurt by a tongue-lashing. As I grow older, I get brief. To see the back of things, I don't always need to have seen the front. I sew by hand and machine. I do not knit. My parents decided to choose my name from among those of three children who appear in little lockets passed down in our family: Armand died crazy in Charenton, Adrien became a painter, thanks to some premonition and hoping to prevent me from going crazy or becoming a painter, they chose Edouard, so I have punctured at least one of their superstitions. I do not work much with a flash because I don't like interruptions. I admire the intelligence of ecological solutions. I do not dream of going on a cruise. I do not use the following expressions: "That rings a bell," "Laters," "Works for me," "That's hot." I do not say to someone I haven't seen in a long time, "What's the word?" When someone talks to me about his or her "energy," I can feel the conversation grinding to a halt. I am afraid of ending up a bum. I am afraid of having my computer and negatives stolen. I cannot tell what, in me, is innate. I do not have a head for business. I do not vary what I serve at dinner parties. I have stepped on a rake and had the handle hit me in the face. I do not follow the advice in guide books, I trust in chance, my intuition, and the advice of the natives. The motto of the collège Stanislas, where I spent fifteen years, is "French without fear, Christian beyond reproach." I have gone to four psychiatrists, one psychologist, one psychotherapist, and five psychoanalysts. I have spent fifteen days in a psychiatric hospital and every week, for months, I checked into another psychiatric hospital. I look for the simple things I no longer see. I do not go to confession. Legs slightly open excite me more than legs wide open. I have trouble forbidding. I am not mature. Australia attracts me no more and no less than Canada. I used to love shells, pocket knives, truncheons, and other army surplus. Sunstroke makes me hot on the outside and cold on the inside. I am leery of movies adapted from novels, and of novels adapted from movies. I don't get off on possession. I don't remember what I saw when I emerged from the womb. Sergeant Garcia made all sergeants seem comical to me. I spent a year languishing because I didn't travel. I appreciate the simplicity of Biblical language. I vote. I live better in two houses than in one. I appreciate swingers' clubs, which take the logic of the nightclub to its natural conclusion. I was five years old when a clown said, "And now I'm going to ask a little boy to come up on stage," there was a drumroll and the spotlight fell on me, when the clown came toward me, I cried so fiercely that he turned to another child. I have had the measles, the mumps, and chicken pox. I have seen an eagle. I have seen starfish. I learned to draw by copying pornographic photographs. I have a foggy sense of history, and of stories in general, chronology bores me. I do not suffer from the absence of those I love. I prefer desire to pleasure. My death will change nothing. I would like to write in a language not my own. I consent to feeling moved by sunsets. Abundance leaves me bewildered. There is no age I admire. I can do without the interludes, but I appreciate the preliminaries. I find tips humiliating for the giver and the receiver. After I get a haircut, my hair's too short. The speed of a cheetah still amazes me. I like to have habits, then suddenly change them. I don't show up early because I don't like to wait. Waiting doesn't bother me if I expected it, but that's not really waiting. I don't like to order or be ordered around. I editorialize. I move on. When I was a child, I didn't ask riddles. I don't know how many animals I could recognize by scent. To survive an ordeal, I break it up into sections. I cannot remember having spoken to a New Zealander. I improvise only at the piano. Despite myself, I look away when I pass a dwarf. I hear the word "marvelous" and I marvel. I do not use the word "gamine." As far as I know, only one woman has gotten pregnant by me.

Borrowing is an ordeal. They took out four wisdom teeth, unless maybe it was two. Because of their names, certain acts strike me as outdated, for example, "laying down a deposit." Tonsils (*amygdales*) make me think of spiders (*mygales*). I have come in mouths. I have come on faces. I have come in pussies. I have come on breasts. I have come in hands. I have come on pubes. I have come on bellies. I have come on and in asses. I have come on backs. I have come in hair. I have come on thighs. In the moment, I suffer less from a big shock than a small one. There are words that I always use with some other word, for example, "aforethought." I do not notice earrings, necklaces, rings, and bracelets except to disapprove. Diamonds and fur coats put me off. I ask for several estimates. I don't regret not having been revealed. I don't mind giving a Christmas bonus but I don't want a free calendar. I will gladly pay musicians in restaurants to stop playing. I do not wait for a sale to buy. The word "titbit" somehow makes me think of pedophilia. When I look at a strawberry, I think of a tongue, when I lick one, of a kiss. I can see how drops of water could be torture. A burn on my tongue has a taste. My memories, good or bad, are sad the way dead things are sad. A friend can let me down but not an enemy. I ask the price before I buy. I go nowhere with my eyes closed. When I was a child I had bad taste in music. Playing sports bores me after an hour. Laughing unarouses me. Often, I wish it were tomorrow. My memory is structured like a disco ball. I wonder if there are still parents around to threaten their children with a whipping. The voice, the lyrics, and the face of Daniel Darc made French rock listenable to me. The best conversations I had date from adolescence, with a friend at whose place we drank cocktails that we made by mixing up his mother's liquor at random, we would talk until sunrise in the salon of that big house where Mallarmé had once been a guest, in the course of those nights I delivered speeches on love, politics, God, and death of which I retain not one word, even though sometimes I came up with them doubled over in laughter, years later, this friend told his wife that he had left something in the house just as they were going to play tennis, he went down to the basement and put a bullet in his head with the gun he had carefully prepared. I have memories of comets with powdery tails. I read the dictionary. I went into a glass labyrinth called the Palace of Mirrors. I wonder where the dreams go that I don't remember. I do not know what to do with my hands when they have nothing to do. Even though it's not for me, I turn around when someone whistles in the street. Dangerous animals do not scare me. I have seen lightening. I wish they had slides for grown-ups. I have read more volumes one than volumes two. The date on my birth certificate is wrong. I am not sure I have any influence. I talk to my things when they're sad. I don't know why I write. I prefer a ruin to a monument. I am calm during reunions. I have nothing against New Year's Eve. Fifteen years old is the middle of my life, regardless of when I die. I believe there is an afterlife, but not an afterdeath. I do not ask "do you love me." Only once can I say "I'm dying" without telling a lie. The best day of my life may already be behind me.

EDOUARD LEVÉ was born on January 1, 1965, in Neuilly-sur-Seine. A writer, photographer, and visual artist, Levé was the author of four books of prose—*Oeuvres, Journal, Auto-portrait,* and *Suicide*—and three books of photographs. He took his own life in 2007.

LORIN STEIN is editor of *The Paris Review.*

SELECTED DALKEY ARCHIVE PAPERBACKS

FOR A FULL LIST OF PUBLICATIONS, VISIT:
www.dalkeyarchive.com

SELECTED DALKEY ARCHIVE PAPERBACKS

Man in the Holocene.
CARLOS FUENTES, *Christopher Unborn.*
  Distant Relations.
  Terra Nostra.
  Where the Air Is Clear.
WILLIAM GADDIS, *J R.*
  The Recognitions.
JANICE GALLOWAY, *Foreign Parts.*
  The Trick Is to Keep Breathing.
WILLIAM H. GASS, *Cartesian Sonata
    and Other Novellas.*
  Finding a Form.
  A Temple of Texts.
  The Tunnel.
  Willie Masters' Lonesome Wife.
GÉRARD GAVARRY, *Hoppla! 1 2 3.*
  Making a Novel.
ETIENNE GILSON,
  The Arts of the Beautiful.
  Forms and Substances in the Arts.
C. S. GISCOMBE, *Giscome Road.*
  Here.
  Prairie Style.
DOUGLAS GLOVER, *Bad News of the Heart.*
  The Enamoured Knight.
WITOLD GOMBROWICZ,
  A Kind of Testament.
KAREN ELIZABETH GORDON,
  The Red Shoes.
GEORGI GOSPODINOV, *Natural Novel.*
JUAN GOYTISOLO, *Count Julian.*
  Exiled from Almost Everywhere.
  Juan the Landless.
  Makbara.
  Marks of Identity.
PATRICK GRAINVILLE, *The Cave of Heaven.*
HENRY GREEN, *Back.*
  Blindness.
  Concluding.
  Doting.
  Nothing.
JACK GREEN, *Fire the Bastards!*
JIŘÍ GRUŠA, *The Questionnaire.*
GABRIEL GUDDING,
  Rhode Island Notebook.
MELA HARTWIG, *Am I a Redundant
    Human Being?*
JOHN HAWKES, *The Passion Artist.*
  Whistlejacket.
ALEKSANDAR HEMON, ED.,
  Best European Fiction.
AIDAN HIGGINS, *A Bestiary.*
  Balcony of Europe.
  Bornholm Night-Ferry.
  Darkling Plain: Texts for the Air.
  Flotsam and Jetsam.
  Langrishe, Go Down.
  Scenes from a Receding Past.
  Windy Arbours.
KEIZO HINO, *Isle of Dreams.*
KAZUSHI HOSAKA, *Plainsong.*
ALDOUS HUXLEY, *Antic Hay.*
  Crome Yellow.
  Point Counter Point.
  Those Barren Leaves.
  Time Must Have a Stop.
NAOYUKI II, *The Shadow of a Blue Cat.*
MIKHAIL IOSSEL AND JEFF PARKER, EDS.,
  *Amerika: Russian Writers View the
    United States.*
DRAGO JANČAR, *The Galley Slave.*
GERT JONKE, *The Distant Sound.*

Geometric Regional Novel.
  Homage to Czerny.
  The System of Vienna.
JACQUES JOUET, *Mountain R.*
  Savage.
  Upstaged.
CHARLES JULIET, *Conversations with
    Samuel Beckett and Bram van
    Velde.*
MIEKO KANAI, *The Word Book.*
YORAM KANIUK, *Life on Sandpaper.*
HUGH KENNER, *The Counterfeiters.*
  *Flaubert, Joyce and Beckett:
    The Stoic Comedians.*
  Joyce's Voices.
DANILO KIŠ, *Garden, Ashes.*
  A Tomb for Boris Davidovich.
ANITA KONKKA, *A Fool's Paradise.*
GEORGE KONRÁD, *The City Builder.*
TADEUSZ KONWICKI, *A Minor Apocalypse.*
  The Polish Complex.
MENIS KOUMANDAREAS, *Koula.*
ELAINE KRAF, *The Princess of 72nd Street.*
JIM KRUSOE, *Iceland.*
EWA KURYLUK, *Century 21.*
EMILIO LASCANO TEGUI, *On Elegance
    While Sleeping.*
ERIC LAURRENT, *Do Not Touch.*
HERVÉ LE TELLIER, *The Sextine Chapel.*
  *A Thousand Pearls (for a Thousand
    Pennies)*
VIOLETTE LEDUC, *La Bâtarde.*
EDOUARD LEVÉ, *Autoportrait.*
  Suicide.
SUZANNE JILL LEVINE, *The Subversive
    Scribe: Translating Latin
    American Fiction.*
DEBORAH LEVY, *Billy and Girl.*
  *Pillow Talk in Europe and Other
    Places.*
JOSÉ LEZAMA LIMA, *Paradiso.*
ROSA LIKSOM, *Dark Paradise.*
OSMAN LINS, *Avalovara.*
  The Queen of the Prisons of Greece.
ALF MAC LOCHLAINN,
  The Corpus in the Library.
  Out of Focus.
RON LOEWINSOHN, *Magnetic Field(s).*
MINA LOY, *Stories and Essays of Mina Loy.*
BRIAN LYNCH, *The Winner of Sorrow.*
D. KEITH MANO, *Take Five.*
MICHELINE AHARONIAN MARCOM,
  The Mirror in the Well.
BEN MARCUS,
  The Age of Wire and String.
WALLACE MARKFIELD,
  Teitlebaum's Window.
  To an Early Grave.
DAVID MARKSON, *Reader's Block.*
  Springer's Progress.
  Wittgenstein's Mistress.
CAROLE MASO, *AVA.*
LADISLAV MATEJKA AND KRYSTYNA
  POMORSKA, EDS.,
  *Readings in Russian Poetics:
    Formalist and Structuralist Views.*
HARRY MATHEWS,
  *The Case of the Persevering Maltese:
    Collected Essays.*
  Cigarettes.
  The Conversions.
  The Human Country: New and

FOR A FULL LIST OF PUBLICATIONS, VISIT:
www.dalkeyarchive.com

Collected Stories.
The Journalist.
My Life in CIA.
Singular Pleasures.
The Sinking of the Odradek
  Stadium.
Tlooth.
20 Lines a Day.
JOSEPH MCELROY,
  Night Soul and Other Stories.
THOMAS MCGONIGLE,
  Going to Patchogue.
ROBERT L. MCLAUGHLIN, ED., *Innovations:*
  An Anthology of
    Modern & Contemporary Fiction.
ABDELWAHAB MEDDEB, *Talismano.*
GERHARD MEIER, *Isle of the Dead.*
HERMAN MELVILLE, *The Confidence-Man.*
AMANDA MICHALOPOULOU, *I'd Like.*
STEVEN MILLHAUSER,
  The Barnum Museum.
  In the Penny Arcade.
RALPH J. MILLS, JR.,
  Essays on Poetry.
MOMUS, *The Book of Jokes.*
CHRISTINE MONTALBETTI, *Western.*
OLIVE MOORE, *Spleen.*
NICHOLAS MOSLEY, *Accident.*
  Assassins.
  Catastrophe Practice.
  Children of Darkness and Light.
  Experience and Religion.
  God's Hazard.
  The Hesperides Tree.
  Hopeful Monsters.
  Imago Bird.
  Impossible Object.
  Inventing God.
  Judith.
  Look at the Dark.
  Natalie Natalia.
  Paradoxes of Peace.
  Serpent.
  Time at War.
  The Uses of Slime Mould:
    Essays of Four Decades.
WARREN MOTTE,
  Fables of the Novel: French Fiction
    since 1990.
  Fiction Now: The French Novel in
    the 21st Century.
  Oulipo: A Primer of Potential
    Literature.
GERALD MURNANE, *Barley Patch.*
YVES NAVARRE, *Our Share of Time.*
  Sweet Tooth.
DOROTHY NELSON, *In Night's City.*
  Tar and Feathers.
ESHKOL NEVO, *Homesick.*
WILFRIDO D. NOLLEDO, *But for the Lovers.*
FLANN O'BRIEN,
  At Swim-Two-Birds.
  At War.
  The Best of Myles.
  The Dalkey Archive.
  Further Cuttings.
  The Hard Life.
  The Poor Mouth.
  The Third Policeman.
CLAUDE OLLIER, *The Mise-en-Scène.*
  Wert and the Life Without End.
PATRIK OUŘEDNÍK, *Europeana.*

The Opportune Moment, 1855.
BORIS PAHOR, *Necropolis.*
FERNANDO DEL PASO,
  News from the Empire.
  Palinuro of Mexico.
ROBERT PINGET, *The Inquisitory.*
  Mahu or The Material.
  Trio.
A. G. PORTA, *The No World Concerto.*
MANUEL PUIG,
  Betrayed by Rita Hayworth.
  The Buenos Aires Affair.
  Heartbreak Tango.
RAYMOND QUENEAU, *The Last Days.*
  Odile.
  Pierrot Mon Ami.
  Saint Glinglin.
ANN QUIN, *Berg.*
  Passages.
  Three.
  Tripticks.
ISHMAEL REED,
  The Free-Lance Pallbearers.
  The Last Days of Louisiana Red.
  Ishmael Reed: The Plays.
  Juice!
  Reckless Eyeballing.
  The Terrible Threes.
  The Terrible Twos.
  Yellow Back Radio Broke-Down.
JOÃO UBALDO RIBEIRO, *House of the*
  Fortunate Buddhas.
JEAN RICARDOU, *Place Names.*
RAINER MARIA RILKE, *The Notebooks of*
  Malte Laurids Brigge.
JULIÁN RÍOS, *The House of Ulysses.*
  Larva: A Midsummer Night's Babel.
  Poundemonium.
  Procession of Shadows.
AUGUSTO ROA BASTOS, *I the Supreme.*
DANIËL ROBBERECHTS,
  Arriving in Avignon.
JEAN ROLIN, *The Explosion of the*
  Radiator Hose.
OLIVIER ROLIN, *Hotel Crystal.*
ALIX CLEO ROUBAUD, *Alix's Journal.*
JACQUES ROUBAUD, *The Form of a*
  City Changes Faster, Alas, Than
    the Human Heart.
  The Great Fire of London.
  Hortense in Exile.
  Hortense Is Abducted.
  The Loop.
  Mathêmatique:
  The Plurality of Worlds of Lewis.
  The Princess Hoppy.
  Some Thing Black.
LEON S. ROUDIEZ, *French Fiction Revisited.*
RAYMOND ROUSSEL, *Impressions of Africa.*
VEDRANA RUDAN, *Night.*
STIG SÆTERBAKKEN, *Siamese.*
LYDIE SALVAYRE, *The Company of Ghosts.*
  Everyday Life.
  The Lecture.
  Portrait of the Writer as a
    Domesticated Animal.
  The Power of Flies.
LUIS RAFAEL SÁNCHEZ,
  Macho Camacho's Beat.
SEVERO SARDUY, *Cobra & Maitreya.*
NATHALIE SARRAUTE,
  Do You Hear Them?

SELECTED DALKEY ARCHIVE PAPERBACKS

9 781564 787071